WHICH PIE GOES WITH MURDER?

AN IVY CREEK COZY MYSTERY

RUTH BAKER

AN IVY CREEK COZY MYSTERY

BOOK ONE

BOOK ONE

1

$\mathcal{T}$he town hadn't changed much since Lucy's last visit. She noticed this when she arrived at the cemetery earlier that day for her parent's funeral. It was a short ceremony, and she had made most of the plans together with her aunt while she was in Ivy Creek. When she arrived earlier that morning, she had gone straight to the cemetery.

Her aunt drove back to her house in the neighboring town as soon as the ceremony was over, and Lucy headed back home. The first thing Lucy noticed as she arrived at her parent's house was that the front lawn was still as beautifully kept as ever. Her mother had always paid special attention to it. She had loved the beautiful burst of flowers that bloomed, especially in the summer, and Lucy had grown to love that effect too.

She got out of her car and looked around the yard, unable to wrap her mind around the death of her parents. It was sudden, painful, and destabilizing. It'd been a few days, but she already missed them.

This town, Ivy Creek, was not a place for her, and she

hoped she wouldn't have to stay in town for a day longer than necessary. She had moved to the city years ago, where she had carved out a life for herself, and she was thriving there. This tragedy was the only thing bringing her back to town.

As she walked towards the front door of the house, she turned around when she heard a dog bark. She saw the next-door neighbor, Maureen Jones, a woman Lucy remembered from when she was little, walk past holding her dog on a leash.

"Lucy, dear," the woman's edgy voice boomed, the corners of her lips lifted in a smile.

Lucy forced a smile onto her face and turned around to greet Maureen.

"It's a surprise to see you in town, and a tragedy what happened to your parents. They were such a lovely couple."

Lucy greeted her with a peck on both cheeks and stepped back.

"I hope you are handling everything fine?"

"Yes, I am," she replied with another smile. "Thank you, Mrs. Jones."

The woman nodded and pulled on the leash of her dog as she walked away. Lucy turned around and walked to the house. She went right to the flower pot at the corner of the front porch, took the keys from under it, and slipped it into the keyhole to open the door.

Once inside, she looked around, and a wave of nostalgia hit her. Tears instantly filled her eyes. The last time she was here, it was Christmas, three years ago. She had made it just in time for the traditional family dinner after her mother had nagged her about it for weeks.

She felt an instant wave of guilt overwhelm her for caring less about her parents these past years. *This is my home. I grew up here, but now it feels different... empty.*

I should have visited more often.

She sucked in a deep breath, headed for the stairs in the corner. Upstairs, Lucy looked around, taking in the perfect arrangements of the smaller living room. The pictures of her when she was younger hanging on the walls, and more of her dad holding her when she had won her first award in high school on the girl's sprinting team.

Lucy wiped at her eyes gently, then took a short tour around the rest of the house. Her old bedroom was still the same, her pictures hung on the wall, and her closet remained untouched. The wallpapers she had loved so much still hung on the walls.

She dropped on the bed, and gently stroked the sheets with her hands, then sniffed. "I'm so sorry mom, and dad. I should have been here more often," she muttered to herself.

In a few hours, she would be hosting guests in the bakery, and she didn't feel like she was up to it, but she dragged herself off the bed. She spent time staring at her reflection in the full-length mirror by the corner of her bed, then went into her closet to find a pair of jeans and a T-shirt that still fit. She grabbed the keys to the bakery from her parent's room and headed out.

The drive to the bakery on one of Ivy Creek's high streets was short. The outside remained the same, with its Norman Rockwell like painting. The inside was arranged in a pattern that drew the customers to the right side where the display glasses were, and a huge menu hung on the wall, listing everything they made. Minutes later, she was inside, cleaning up and gathering baking supplies from the shelves she could use to prepare snacks for her guests. She went into the storage room and came back with everything she needed in a large bowl, then went ahead to prepare a mixture for blueberry streusel muffins and cookies.

Lucy used her mother's recipes she had learned when she

was younger. She used to enjoy helping her out in the bakery a lot back then, and watching her parents work together had been fun. It was why she had successfully carved out a career in food blogging for herself and trying out new recipes was a favorite for her.

Lucy sat in the kitchen and waited after putting her dough into the oven. The bakery was still intact, and for a moment, she wondered what would happen now that they were gone. They had put so much effort and dedication into running the bakery for years, and Sweet Delights had thrived because of that.

The creamy and comforting scent of vanilla she had used in her dough filled the atmosphere, alerting her that her muffins were baked into a perfectly brown color, and as she took them out, and put in the next set, a soft knock on the front door told her the first guest had arrived.

———

IN ABOUT AN HOUR, the bakery was filled with citizens of Ivy Creek, some of whom Lucy recognized. They were all pleasant, chatting lightly amongst themselves as they enjoyed the confectionaries she had baked. She was proud she was able to pull it off in a few hours. Cleaning the bakery hadn't been hard at all as it was hardly ever dirty, and the majority of the work had been baking the pastries.

Lucy greeted an old friend of her father's briefly with a handshake, engaged in a light conversation with him for a few minutes before moving on to anyone else she recognized. Half an hour into the meeting, the door to the bakery opened again, and Lucy's heart did a slow dive in her chest as she noticed the man who walked in through the door. He was dressed in a black shirt tucked into navy blue jeans, and she didn't miss the gun belt on his waist. Lucy knew he had always wanted to go into law enforcement and could see he did it.

She swallowed as his eyes scanned the room, then settled on her. They stared at each other for a brief moment, and the only thing Lucy could think of at that moment was that in the five years since she last saw him, he hadn't changed one bit.

Of course, he had aged a little. His once boyish looks were gone and had been replaced with stubble that covered his face. Their gaze locked for a moment before he walked towards her. Lucy sipped from the glass she held and cleared her throat when he arrived and stood in front of her, slipping his hands into his pocket.

"Lucy Hale," he said in a low voice, his pale blue eyes not leaving hers. "It took a tragedy to bring you back home."

His statement was flat, with an underlying meaning they both understood, and Lucy plastered a smile on her face and extended a hand to him. He hesitated at first, but then slowly accepted the gesture.

"Taylor Baker—it's a pleasant surprise to have you here," she replied, and he cocked a brow. His gaze roamed her face again, and Lucy knew from the look in his eyes that he had not forgotten their history.

Taylor released her hand and slipped his back into his pocket. "Mr. and Mrs. Hale were friends of my parents too, and they are here, so it's only right that I pay my respects."

Lucy nodded, and just then Taylor's mother found them and greeted Lucy with a big hug. "Hello, Mrs. Baker."

"We are so sorry for your loss, dear," Taylor's mother whispered to her and took both her hands in hers. "It's a tragedy what happened to Morris and Kareen. They were such lovely people, the accident was a true loss for every one of us."

"Thank you," Lucy replied gently with a smile again, and

Taylor whispered something to his mother before she walked away.

"So, you running again as soon as this is over?" he asked casually. "We both know Ivy Creek does not suit your exquisite needs," he added.

Her mind prepared a snappy reply to his question, but she suppressed it and nodded instead.

She didn't have the strength to get into an argument with Taylor, not at a gathering hosted in honor of her parents. All she wanted was for the night to be over, so she could slip into her bed and sleep for a long time. She was exhausted, partly because she had to stand here and accept condolences from almost everyone in town.

The gathering was her aunt's idea, and she wasn't even here to attend it because she had to get back to her daughter, who just had a baby back home.

"I don't think I'll stay," Lucy replied with a small smile, ignoring the contempt she saw in his eyes.

"I didn't think you would."

Three years ago, the Christmas she had visited, she ran into Taylor at the grocery store, and his attitude had been the same. Even though she had tried to apologize to him then, too. Lucy knew she didn't need to apologize every time they ran into each other. They had shared history, and she had chosen to move on for the sake of her career. If he couldn't forgive her for that, then there was little she could do about it.

"Thanks for paying your respects, Taylor. I appreciate it. I have to go now... to talk to other guests," she said, emptying the contents of her glass as she walked away from him, aware that his gaze was pinned on her the entire time.

She stole glances at him as he moved to join his parents in the corner of the bakery. She saw him join their conversation, and as he picked up one muffin and took a bite, she waited to see the reaction on his face.

He had enjoyed her baking once, when they were together, and he complimented it far too many times. She couldn't tell if he still thought it was good enough, and before she could look away, his gaze found hers across the room again, and lingered. He looked away first, and Lucy turned and focused on the conversation with her guests.

By the end of the gathering, Lucy cleaned up the place alone and finished late. She didn't want to go back to the main house tonight. The place held a lot of memories of her happy life there and it was painful to stay there alone.

She remembered there was a small apartment above the bakery, and as she closed the doors to the main entrance and locked the back exit, she hoped it would come in handy for her for the night. Lucy went up the stairs and flipped the light switch on, and the first thing she saw was her mother's cat, Gigi, huddled in a corner.

She bent over and touched its head as it came towards her. She let her gaze travel around the small living space, and she smiled. "This is better than I remember, and it'll be perfect."

She went in to check the bedrooms; there were two of them. It was more than enough for the night, or as long as she wished to stay. She made a trip downstairs to grab her luggage in her car, parked in the backyard. After closing her doors, she retired back to the living room upstairs to comfort herself with a cup of chamomile tea, hoping it would ease the stress of what had been quite an eventful day.

Seeing the number of locals who turned up in honor of her parents surprised her, and Taylor's presence too had shocked her, but his usual cold attitude hadn't. He was never going to forgive her. She had come to terms with that, and she could handle it.

As Lucy fell asleep, she hoped that time would heal the heaviness in her heart from her loss. When she opened her eyes the next morning, it was to the sound of something clattering downstairs. Lucy jumped out of her bed, and her heartbeat skyrocketed, leaving her with a rush of adrenaline that produced a tight knot in the pit of her stomach.

Who was out there?

2

*A*s Lucy made her way towards the door, she grabbed a baseball bat she found in the corner of her room. And as she tiptoed down the stairs, different thoughts raced through her mind. Several things could have produced that sound, and she hoped it was not someone trying to burgle her.

Holding a baseball bat was a stupid idea. She could not defend herself from a burglar with a bat if they had a gun. She realized this and chastised herself as she climbed down the stairs, her heart pounding in her chest. When she pushed the adjoining door to the bakery and peered in, relief flooded her instantly.

Gigi, her mother's Persian cat, sat in front of the door, staring at an empty tin plate Lucy suspected made the sound that woke her up. She sighed and stared at the clean white cat and it meowed at her as she bent over to pick it up. Lucy had always loved her blue eyes the most, and she rubbed Gigi's belly as she purred.

"You scared me, Gigi," she whispered to her as she ruffled

its fur and took it into the kitchen. "When did you slip out? And how did you stay down there alone all night?"

Lucy suspected Gigi must have followed her down the stairs when she went to grab her luggage, and when she returned, she had forgotten to check on her because she had fallen asleep on the couch after her cup of tea. "Let's fix your breakfast."

She took Gigi to the kitchen, placed her on the floor gently, and reached into the top of the refrigerator for a bottle of water. While Gigi drank the water, she fixed herself a bowl of cereal and made a mental note of the groceries she needed in the house.

Lucy wasn't certain how long she would be staying yet, but she still needed the supplies. After finishing her cereal, she took a shower, dressed in a pair of slacks and a red sweatshirt, then walked out to the nearest grocery store just around the corner.

The woman at the counter remembered Lucy the moment she walked into the store, and she waved at her with a huge smile.

"How have you been, Keisha?" she asked as she walked past her, and Keisha's response was as hearty as her smile.

Lucy went around the store, picking up toiletries and food items for the kitchen. She walked past the pet area and picked out a nail clipper for Gigi as she had noticed earlier that her claws were untrimmed. As she turned to walk to the counter, she bumped into someone.

"Oh... I'm so sorry," she blurted and raised her head to stare into the cold blue eyes of the man blocking her path. "Forgive me," she added, and stepped to the side to walk past him, but he blocked her again.

"You must be Lucy Hale," he said, and squinted his eyes. A slow smile spread on his lips, and the hairs on the back of her neck stood as she stared at his icy blue eyes.

"I'm Dennis Fischer—I own Spring's Bakery on First Avenue."

Lucy smiled after he introduced himself, even though she couldn't recall the town having another bakery. As far as she knew, Sweet Delights was the only bakery in town. "I'm sorry... I haven't been in town for a long time, so I'm not used to the new places yet."

"I've run Springs for three years," he continued, ignoring her outstretched hand, and Lucy tucked it back to her side. "It's not new."

"Right."

"I heard about your parents' accident. I'm truly sorry about what happened," he said, and she got the slightest feeling that he was not sorry. She ignored it, and nodded, then politely excused herself so she could walk to the counter.

Dennis's words stopped her halfway. "You're not planning to stay in town, are you?"

She turned back to face him. "Is there a reason I shouldn't?"

He walked menacingly towards her. "There isn't," he replied. "But your parents and I were on our way to finalizing a deal that would make Sweet Delights a subsidiary of Springs."

Lucy had to laugh at that because she knew her parents would never sell Sweet Delights. It was their legacy; an embodiment of everything they had worked for. Why would they sell off when they weren't facing any issues?

"I sincerely doubt that," she replied. "I have to head out now," she added. "Have a nice day, Dennis."

"Watch your back, Lucy," he said.

She ignored him and walked to the counter. As Keisha entered her items into the system, Lucy bit her lower lip and pondered on Dennis's statement. *Could he be telling the truth?*

"I see you met Dennis Fischer," Keisha said, her wide eyes roaming the store.

"I did, and he is not a very nice man."

Keisha cleared her throat and handed over the bag of items to Lucy. "He is one of the town's richest and his reputation is formidable. I think he's rude," Keisha said as she punched keys on the cash register. "That will be fifty bucks."

Lucy paid her in cash. "Have you ever visited his bakery?"

"Yes… Although Dennis is a jerk, Springs is the finest bakery in town. I won't deny that the man has got good taste with all that interior décor and lighting, makes it look more like one of those fancy coffee spots in the city. Perhaps when you have the time, you could try out his tarts, they simply melt in your mouth."

Lucy smiled at her. "I will. Thank you, Keisha," she said and walked away from the counter. As she slipped out of the store, she caught Dennis's gaze on her through the glass door and noticed his jaw tighten as he watched her.

———

Lucy couldn't hide her curiosity, so later that evening, she located Springs Bakery and tried out the tarts Keisha had recommended. When she took the first bite, she moaned and had to admit it was awesome.

The place was lively; the interior was decorated with bright hues of green and flower wallpapers at the edges of the wall. Outside, there was a patio, with chairs and tables arranged in a rectangular form, and beautiful flowers on the decks.

She had to admit that the man had good taste. His workers were organized and polite in attending to their customers. She noticed the woman behind the counter always had a smile plastered on her face.

Lucy remembered her mother's words about hospitality as she watched the chef. *"It is easier to retain customers if they think you are hospitable, Lucy. Never forget that."*

Lucy ordered an apple pie when she was done with the tart and took it alongside a freshly made strawberry juice. When she finished eating, she left the place and strolled back home.

Dennis ran a fine business, but he lacked fine manners. Her mother would have been very clear with a man like him about that, so she was positive her parents never planned to sell Sweet Delights. Besides, if there was a reason to sell or a pending deal, the lawyers would have mentioned it when she finalized every detail of their life insurance and property with him.

They had willed her the bakery, and the house, and she was yet to decide what she wanted to do with them. Maybe one day, she might quit her job at the media house she worked for and come back here to plant roots? She couldn't tell because that would be a long time from now, but she was certain she wouldn't sell out. As she strolled, she recognized Taylor's house when she neared it, and just then he drove his truck slowly from the adjoining road leading to her street, past her, and swerved into his parking space.

She paused when he got out of his car and walked over to where she stood.

"You're still in town?" he asked, and Lucy nodded.

"I figured I could stay a few more days and see what I can do around here."

He laughed and crossed his arms over his chest. "There is nothing you can do around here. The town's too small for a girl like you, remember?"

His cynicism made her roll her eyes. "Come on, Taylor. Enough of your judgmental attitude. I could use a break from it."

"I am being honest, not judgmental. We both know you don't want to be around here and would rather go back to your big-shot media job in the city. That suits you more than flour-covered jeans and getting your hands dirty doing a real job."

"And what if I decide to stay?" she asked, and crossed her arms over her chest, raising her head defiantly. "I own the bakery now, and I grew up working there. Who says I wouldn't do a good job running it?"

"You wouldn't," he replied with a shrug, his brown eyes fixed on hers, so she could see how serious he was. "I don't think you can manage it, and when it gets tough, you'll probably run, anyway."

Lucy opened her mouth to say something, but snapped it shut again. Her eyes flared, and she bit her lower lip.

"Well, I have decided to stay," she replied, and the momentary drop in his jaw gave her satisfaction. *How dare he tell me what I can and can't do?*

"Sweet Delights is my family's legacy, and I will stay and see it through, no matter what you or anyone else thinks."

She expected him to say something else to kill her zeal, but he pressed his lips together, turned away from her, and walked into his house without another word. Lucy stood in front of his house for a few more seconds before turning and walking down the road, heading back home.

She grew up in this town and Sweet Delights was her inheritance, so she would take care of it in her parent's stead. *How hard could that be?*

It was a challenge, and she loved challenges… it was the reason she moved to the city in the first place. It had posed something new and thrilling, and she had gone for it. She believed she could become more than a small-town girl, living in her parent's nest her entire life.

She hadn't regretted her decision to live and work in

Denver, not even for one day, and she didn't think she would regret this choice either. She could give running the bakery a try. *What's the harm in staying a few more weeks?*

Lucy sent in a letter to her manager at work before she went to bed, telling him she was needed to stay back in Ivy Creek for a few more weeks. As she hit the send button, she felt the first shiver of anticipation run down her spine. She walked to her window and stared out into the night filled with stars, admiring the beauty of the horizon, and the peak of the mountains teetering far into the sky, far from where her house stood.

"I hope I can do this, mom," she whispered to herself and closed her eyes. "I hope I can handle it without ruining everything you and dad worked hard for."

3

*R*unning a bakery is not a piece of cake. Lucy knew this, so the next morning, the first thing she did was to put out a 'help wanted' sign. She cleaned out the inside of the bakery, wiped the windows clean and rearranged the chairs in a more suitable pattern.

When she had first started a food blog, it had been a crazy idea she didn't think would amount to much. The first few months proved she could do better if she was consistent, and that principle was what she applied to everything she did.

Lucy did a quick inspection of the bakery, satisfied that the walls were still good enough. She paid little attention to changing the wallpaper or stripping away the decorative mosaic she had made as a little girl hanging on the left side of the kitchen wall. Instead, she focused on making sure every inch of the store and kitchen was dusted out.

As she inspected the chimney inside the kitchen where the large industrial oven lay, she whistled to herself a familiar song she learned as a child. Gigi followed her around the bakery, making little purrs whenever she wanted to be noticed, and Lucy constantly flashed her a smile. She had always loved the idea of having a pet, but she never kept one because she was never in the house. Lucy's job required regular visits to different cities so she could keep her blog active and trending with the latest news and recipes on food.

In the last article she had published weeks before her parent's death, she had mentioned lots of native American dishes to try out, some of which she might include in the Sweet Delights menu.

She smiled to herself as she thought of all the amazing things she could do to generate more sales and publicity for the bakery. It felt like she could excel at this already, and she hadn't even begun yet.

By the end of the second day, she had completely cleaned the place and checked the equipment in the bakery for any that needed replacing. It was on the second day she got the first applicant for the position of a chef she had displayed out front. As Lucy sat in front of the red-haired teenager, she smiled, trying to appear warm and welcoming even though she could tell the girl knew nothing about baking.

"Hi, I'm Samantha, but most people just call me Sam," the girl said.

"I'm Lucy," she replied. "Do you enjoy baking?"

Samantha chuckled, then shrugged, and Lucy watched as she admired her nails individually.

"I don't have the slightest idea what baking is about," she replied, laughing. "Mom says I should get a job, and I have to admit, blueberry scones have always fascinated me. I love them. I love eating them."

Lucy had to laugh at the girl's facial expressions while she talked and crossed her out in her mind. They talked some more about her experimental baking, and Lucy had to end the interview early when another applicant strolled into the bakery.

The second applicant was a tall man, older than Lucy

would have loved to hire, but witty and smart. He spent half the time cracking jokes about his experience in restaurants in town and then told her about his allergy to vanilla.

Another applicant walked in after she had finished her lunch.

"Do you have any prior knowledge of baking?" Lucy asked and listened as the woman explained baking cakes for dessert. She interchanged the steps, and if anyone was to bake using the steps she highlighted, they would end up with nothing close to a cake. She didn't even want to imagine what it would taste like.

Stifling a giggle, she dismissed the woman. "Thanks for applying, Tricia, but I would like to hire someone with good knowledge or interest in the field," she explained with a pleasant smile.

Lucy didn't want to make a mistake in the first stages of running the business by choosing the wrong candidate, not when she had strong competition like Dennis Fischer in town.

She spent the entire day interviewing just three appli-cants, and by the time she put the sign back out the next morning, she hoped she would have better luck. Lucy stood outside for a while, looking at the bakery.

Its exterior reminded her of a five-star restaurant she had blogged about in the city. She wondered if Sweet Delights would ever get to a point where it would garner international reviews, and if it did, could she still maintain this spot on the high street her parents had started the busi-ness on?

Lost in her thoughts, she didn't hear the footsteps of a person who came up behind her until she felt a gentle tap on her shoulder. She spun around and was met with a grin on the girl's face.

"Hi," the girl said in a pleasant voice and extended her hand. "Hannah Curry," she said, her grin not fading.

Lucy stared at the girl, trying to place the face and the smile.

"You're Lucy, right? My God, the rumors are true, you look... different."

When Lucy kept staring at her in a confused state, Hannah pulled her hand away and chuckled. "You were in my senior class at Creek High. We played on the same basketball team for three years, remember?"

Lucy could finally place the face when Hannah mentioned the high school she attended, and she laughed. "Hannah... wow, you look... different yourself," she exclaimed, and spread her arms out for a hug.

Lucy led Hannah into the store, and as they entered, Gigi wiggled her short tail and rushed to Lucy's leg. She purred and lay flat on her back. Whenever she did that, Lucy remembered her mother always rubbed her stomach, so she bent over and did that, allowing her hands to fluff the fur on Gigi's body.

Satisfied, Gigi sashayed across the room, and Lucy offered Hannah a seat.

"Wow, this place hasn't changed," Hannah began as she looked around. "I used to get a lot of pastries from your mom."

"You haven't been in town much?"

Hannah nodded. "Just got back from Texas, and my dad mentioned what happened. When I walked by here a few days back, you weren't around, so I couldn't come in to say hello. It's a tragedy what happened," Hannah added.

"It's so nice of you to come around," Lucy replied. "I appreciate it."

"I see you have a sign out for hire. You plan on running the bakery?"

Lucy nodded, and Hannah sighed, and placed her hand on her chest. "I need a job to keep me busy so I can assist my dad, and baking happens to be something I'm good at."

"I didn't know that," Lucy said and reached for the file on the table in front of her. Inside it, she had made a list of the qualities she wanted in the worker she'd hire for the job.

"I do it as a hobby mostly, and I could learn more from you if you hire me."

"Will you be in town for a long time?"

"I'm back to stay," she replied. "Being in Texas didn't work out as well as I expected, so I came back."

Lucy scanned her notes. She wanted someone she could get along with, a fast learner, and someone pleasant. She had known Hannah for a long time. She also knew her parents, and they seemed like very nice people. "One last thing," Lucy said. "Any food allergies? You would try out a lot of samples while working here and I'd like to know."

"None," she replied. "I like it here, and I think this job will be good for me."

Lucy smiled at her. "You have the job," she said, after crossing out the list she made. She had spent the last two days interviewing applicants who wasted her time, and she was eager to move to the next phase in growing her business.

"You don't need me to do anything else?"

Lucy laughed. "Of course not," she closed the file. "You'll be learning most of my recipes anyway, so your knowledge in baking is enough to get you the job."

"When do I start?"

"Tomorrow... I'll make a trip to town to stock up, and then we are set to sail."

4

*T*he local market was close to the bakery and Lucy went out with a comprehensive list to get supplies. Hannah had resumed at the bakery, and today she was ready to sell desserts and pastries to the citizens of Ivy Creek. She had gotten half the items on her list; baking soda, flavors, food colorings, cinnamon, and a smaller mixer she could use in teaching Hannah new cake recipes for their dessert menu.

When she returned to the bakery, Hannah helped in putting away the items. They discussed the menu she had drafted out for each day of the week.

"Do you have any ideas to add to the dessert menu?" Lucy asked.

"Scones, I've always loved them," Hannah replied with a smile.

Lucy loved scones, so she scribbled it down on her notepad and they walked out of the inner storage room together. "Today we should make bread for sale, and tomorrow we can start with other desserts."

"I'll get the items we need," Hannah replied as the door to

the bakery opened. Dennis walked in just as Hannah went into the kitchen, and Lucy walked to meet him as he looked around the place like he was inspecting it. There were some customers inside the bakery, enjoying their pastries, when Dennis walked in, and Lucy noticed the smug look on his face.

"I love what you've done with the place. Although you are lacking in loyal and passionate customers, just like your parents," he said to her, his eyes dancing around her arrangements.

"Thank you. Do you need something?"

He looked at her again and reached into the pocket of the blue suit he wore. Lucy noticed it was an expensive designer suit, and she noticed the platinum ring on his right finger. He handed over an envelope to her.

"I told you your parents were about to sell off this bakery to me. Here is a part payment cashier's check. You should take this and leave town."

Lucy scoffed, took the envelope from him, and looked at the writing on the front. "Ten thousand bucks is a lot of money to get me to leave town," she replied and handed it back to him.

"There is no room for you here, and besides, you don't strike me as the kind of woman who would want to sell pastries in a small town."

She rolled her eyes. "Are you scared of a little competition, Mr. Fischer?" she asked, raising her head in defiance. "This bakery existed before Springs' came to town. Why do you think a few measly dollars will get me to sell out?"

"Anyone can sell out with just the right amount of cash," he replied with a smile Lucy perceived as false. The man was obnoxious and annoying. How did anyone get along with him?

"Well, I'm not selling out, so you might have to get used to having me as your competition, Dennis, and trust me, I will be the last one standing," she replied, and crossed her arms over her chest. "If there is nothing else I can help you with, I suggest you leave my property now."

He nodded, then took a step back. "You'll regret this," he said, then turned around and walked out of the bakery.

Lucy remained in the same spot after he was gone, and when she turned around, her gaze fell on a woman staring at her. Three other customers in the bakery watched as the woman walked over to her and gently placed a hand on her shoulder.

"Maybe you should take the offer, dear," the woman said. "This place has lost its customers to Springs already."

"My parent's bakery existed before Springs," she insisted.

Hannah walked out of the kitchen with a bowl of everything needed to bake the bread, and Lucy proceeded to teach her a recipe for coconut bread.

Lucy had a positive feeling about the bakery. Together with her blogging skills, she could gather more customers this summer, and make more sales. She knew it would shock everyone, and that was what motivated her.

Dennis Fischer might think he ran the best bakery in town, but she was certain soon she would trump his services and make a name for herself.

———

BY THE END of the week, Sweet Delights was in full operation. Customers trooped in often during the day, and in the evenings, some stopped by to have order a late night dessert. She had to visit the local market sooner than she expected to get more supplies, and she ran into Dennis again.

He rolled his cart to where she stood, inspecting the crates of eggs on a stand, and he cleared his throat to gain her attention when she ignored his presence.

"Dennis," she said in an indifferent tone.

"I see you are still in town and making sales. Everyone is talking about you making it till the end of the month. They seem to mention that you left town because you felt the city had more need for talents like yours... What was it again? LFB... Lucy's food blog?"

"Yes, that's my blog," she replied.

"Don't you think blogging suits you better? You could write an article on Springs Bakery. I will pay you handsomely for it." He leaned closer to her and added. "Of course, before you completely ruin Sweet Delights."

Annoyed, Lucy stepped away from him. "Is that a threat? Any more threats Dennis and you'll confirm my impression that you're scared I'll do better than you," she said, suddenly realizing her loud tone had attracted a small crowd.

His smile dropped, and he looked around. People had stopped to watch, and she stepped closer to him.

"I should warn you I'm quite an ambitious woman, Dennis. And I'll not be intimidated by you or anyone else."

Lucy noticed that Dennis' mouth fell open for a moment. He regained his composure and made his way through the crowd. Satisfied that she had rendered him speechless, Lucy rolled her cart away and paid for her items at the counter.

When she returned to the bakery, Hannah was sitting alone on a chair in the small patio they had arranged, and she drove her car to the back of the building, and joined her.

"You won't believe the day I'm having," she said when Hannah pushed an unopened bottle of water to her. She grabbed it and drank half its content, then continued talking as she covered the bottle. "Dennis seems to be more of a jerk than I thought he was."

"Everyone in town knows he is," Hannah replied. "I think there are people who are naturally jerks. Dennis is one of them."

Hannah dropped her voice a notch. "Rumors have it that his wife went nuts putting up with his attitude, and sometimes when it gets bad, he checks her into a nursing home for weeks. She returned home to him and hasn't been in one for months since."

The revelation shocked Lucy. How much had she missed since she was away from town? "He keeps asking me to sell the bakery to him, and I think he's scared that I will be bad for his business."

Hannah laughed. "Anyone who's had your bread will admit that you are strong competition for Dennis."

Lucy smiled. It was nice to have someone encourage her for the first time since she opened up, and if Hannah felt this way, then there might be others who did, too.

They closed the bakery at eight pm, which had always been her parent's closing time, and Lucy retired to bed early after taking stock of the money she had already invested into the bakery. The next morning, she went for a run down the trail from her backyard. The path led to the town's field, and she remembered jogging through it countless times with Taylor in the past.

Standing at the back of the building where she parked her car, Lucy bent over to tie her laces before stepping down. She walked around the house, warming up her legs, and as she approached the small fence surrounding her mother's garden, a stench hit her nostrils.

It was a strong putrid smell similar to that of rotting cabbage. She followed it, wanting to see what it was. Lucy's eyes landed on shoes first, and she bent over to pick them up only to realize it wasn't just shoes, but a full body.

Her eyes landed on the man's pale face, and she fell on her

butt. Terror tore through her as she landed on the ground and scrambled away from the body hurriedly. Her eyes widened, and she screamed in horror at the sight before her.

Dennis Fischer lay cold and lifeless in her backyard.

5

*L*ucy spent half the day in the police station, giving her statement. The officer who took her in had said it was just to give a statement, but what was going on was more of an interrogation.

"Where did you find the body?" the officer asked again, and Lucy groaned.

"I found him in my backyard," she said for the tenth time, and stared wide eyed at the bald officer focused on typing her words into his system. "Do you even believe anything I have said so far?" she asked.

The man shrugged and pushed back in his chair, rising to his feet. "It is my job to take your statement, miss, and not believe your statement," he replied, then walked away.

Lucy sighed and buried her face in her hands. Dennis' pale face flashed across her mind, and she raised her head immediately. *This could cause me a lot of sleepless nights.*

She had hoped she wouldn't have to call her Aunt Tricia for help soon, but it was obvious she couldn't handle this on her own. Lucy was grateful she had called her aunt the minute she got to the station, and she was expecting her any minute.

Footsteps approached the table where she sat, and Lucy raised her head when she heard Taylor's voice. He slammed the files he held on the table in front of her. "You're free to go."

Lucy sighed and jumped out of the chair. "Thank goodness, I was thinking that they were going to keep me here for longer than this," she said and flexed her neck muscles.

Taylor's jaw ticked, and he turned to walk away, but Lucy stopped him.

"Thank you... for helping," she said and slipped her hands into the pocket of the jeans she wore.

"Don't thank me... I filled out some paperwork, and that's it. Maybe what you should try doing is stop meddling and go back to the city."

"Taylor," she said and sighed. "You... you don't think I killed Dennis, do you? I mean, he was just lying there in my backyard and I..." her voice trailed off as she remembered the distant look in Dennis' eyes as she stumbled on his lifeless body.

"Many people heard you arguing the last time you two were seen together, and then he winds up dead in your backyard?"

Lucy scoffed and folded her arms over her chest. She looked around the room where other cops went about their job and fixed her gaze on his. "You're the Sheriff's deputy, so you tell me, if I murdered Dennis, would I call on the cops to come find him in my backyard?"

"I'm not the cop in charge of finding Dennis' killer," he replied. "But I suggest you quit meddling and do whatever it is you want to do before you leave again."

"Why do you keep suggesting that I would leave town?" Lucy said, and he shifted his weight from one foot to the other. "I'm not going anywhere, so when will you stop being mad that I did what was right for me back then?"

"That has nothing to do with this," Taylor replied, raising his voice a notch, and Lucy rolled her eyes. Taylor caught the movement, huffed, and added. "I mean it Lucy... don't do anything."

Her aunt walked towards them and spread her arms out wide when she saw Lucy. Relief flooded her as she hugged her aunt, and Taylor gave Tricia a stiff smile before he turned and walked away from them.

"I am so glad you came," Lucy said to her, and shoved her fingers through her hair. "It was so terrifying being here all by myself the entire day."

"It's a good thing you called, honey," Tricia replied, and gently patted Lucy's hair. "Are you alright? How long did they keep you here? I bet that felt like all day."

"A couple of hours," Lucy replied and glanced at her watch. She groaned inwardly and looked at Tricia. "I didn't get to open up the bakery today, and Hannah would be so worried," she said as Tricia took her hand and led her out of the station.

"You're running the bakery?"

Lucy nodded and looked at her. "I am trying to do my best, but I don't know if I'm out of my depth here."

"What do you mean?"

They got to Tricia's car, and Lucy got into the front passenger's seat. "The man who died was a competitor. Dennis Fischer... he asked me to sell out to him a few times, and I refused," she explained. "I might have said a few things in anger, and now these people think I killed him."

Tricia sighed and started her engine. "I knew Dennis Fischer, and I will tell you this, honey. Many would be glad that he was dead. He ran a fine business, but he wasn't a fine man," she said as she drove off and sped towards the highway leading to the bakery.

Tricia's words rang in Lucy's head, and she wondered who else stood to benefit a lot from Dennis' death. Whatever Taylor or anyone else thought mattered little, because the truth was she hadn't killed Dennis, but someone did, and the killer was still out there.

———

DENNIS' funeral was the third day after Lucy found his body, and she attended the event with Hannah and her aunt. The entire time, she felt people's gaze on her. She tried not to think about it, but it made her self-conscious.

She knew the citizens of Ivy Creek could gossip. She had grown up here and experienced firsthand what it could be like to be the center of such gossip. When her best-friend in high school was involved in a scandal, Lucy had watched her withdraw into a shell. Every time they were in a public place, the murmurs would increase, and so would the stares. And Gina, her friend, had hated it.

Soon Gina had moved out of town with her parents, and Lucy had found it difficult to make a new friend. It was then she met Taylor Baker. He soon replaced the friend she lost, and they became very close.

Tricia drove her back to the bakery after the funeral, and they both walked in on Hannah, checking her phone. Lucy dropped on a chair after her aunt went upstairs, and she exhaled.

"This is exhausting," Hannah said as she emptied her second glass of strawberry milkshake. "Not even a single soul walked in here today, and this is the fifth day," she complained.

Lucy had tried to pretend like this wasn't getting to her,

but she couldn't keep up the pretence. A business was like a living organism, and she had pumped a lot of money into getting the place running again.

"It's not evening yet, someone will come," she said, and continued typing her latest blog update on her laptop. Her aunt sang to herself as she joined them out on the patio and sat next to Hannah.

"Perhaps we should close up and go have fun for the rest of the evening? You both have been at this for the past five days."

"Someone will come," Lucy said again, and Hannah sighed.

She felt both of their gazes on her as she typed, and she raised her head briefly from her screen to look at them. "Fine, we can close up for today and go visit the park if it'll make you feel better," she said.

She was also exhausted from waiting the entire day and doing nothing. "That's better," Tricia said and got up from where she sat. "You're coming with us, right?" she asked Hannah, and Hannah nodded.

Lucy saved her blog post and closed the file. She would edit it later in the night and send it to her proofreader before uploading it. Minutes later, they were in her aunt's car and they drove down to the park on the outskirts of town.

It was a Sunday evening, and many people came to the park to watch their kids play while they enjoyed the cool evening breeze. Lucy remembered visiting the park often too, and every time she came here, she never missed out on the corn dogs, that Big Joe's concession stand sold.

"Want some Big Joe's corn dogs?" she asked Hannah as they strolled, and Hannah shook her head.

"I prefer pretzels, or a jumbo dill pickle with some celery and peanut butter."

Lucy shook her head and giggled. "You sure eat a lot,

don't you?" she asked as she walked over to the stand and stood in line.

She slipped her hands into the pockets of her leather jacket and pulled out a twenty-dollar bill, then rocked back on her heels as she waited for her turn. Lucy turned when she heard a whisper behind her.

"She runs the bakery... the one where the owner of Springs' was murdered," one whispered to the other. "It's all over the news."

Lucy cleared her throat and stepped forward when it was her turn, and Big Joe's huge smile made her smile. Lucy ignored the whispers behind her.

"Lucy, you're really back in town... thought the rumors were just rumors," Joe said and she laughed.

He had earned his name from his size. Joe Pennel was almost seven feet, with looks similar to that of a polar bear. It took a long time before Lucy could get used to his fierce looks, as she always struggled to reconcile how a man who was so tall, with hairy arms the size of an oak tree, could be so gentle and kind.

"Two corn dogs, Joe," she said and he saluted her.

"As always."

"Add a jumbo dill pickle, celery and peanut butter to that, please."

The girls behind her continued to murmur in hushed whispers, and she pretended not to hear.

"How are you?" Joe asked as he handed over her order. "I heard about..." he didn't finish his statement, and Lucy was grateful that at least someone was still sensitive about the recent demise of an Ivy Creek citizen.

"I'm doing alright, Joe. Thanks for asking, but I'm sure the cops will handle it, and clarify everything."

Joe nodded. "You take care then, and I'm sorry about your

parents," he said as she took the pack. "They were nice people."

Lucy exhaled when she finally walked away from the stand, and she glanced back to see the girls' gaze still following her. When she got to Hannah and Tricia, she handed over a corn dog pack to her aunt, and jumbo dill pickle to Hannah.

They took a spot on a bench to watch the children playing with kites on the grass, and Hannah started a conversation with Tricia about the upcoming summer. As they discussed, Lucy couldn't stop her gaze from shifting over to where Big Joe's concession store stood. In the time they sat there, she counted over fifty customers standing in line, and she sighed.

When she first re-opened the bakery, she had at least gotten a few customers, but now no one even ventured around the bakery. *What can I do?*

Her mind was reeling with thoughts of how to turn things around, and she stared at the empty pack on her lap for a long time. An idea finally came to her, and she muttered, "That's it."

"What is that?" Hannah asked, and Lucy raised her gaze to find both her aunt and Hannah staring at her.

"I know a way we can make more sales," she replied and a grin spread out on her lips slowly as the idea lingered in her mind. "A concession store," she said to Hannah.

"Like Big Joe's?" Tricia asked, and Lucy nodded.

"Don't we need consent for that? Like from the council or something?" Hannah chirped in.

"We do, don't we?" Lucy asked Tricia and her aunt nodded.

"It's a crazy idea, but yes, we need a permit for that, and if you're going to get it, then you need a good recommendation. One that comes from a respected member of the town's committee board."

"Like the sheriff's deputy, or the local priest of the church," Hannah chirped in, and Lucy groaned as she realized to get started on this new idea, she might need help from Taylor Baker. He was the town's sheriff's deputy and was also the last person who would be inclined to help her.

6

"Yⁱou think my idea is terrible?" Lucy asked her aunt as she sat in the living room above the bakery. She had called Taylor three times since she had her concession stand idea, and each time it went to his voice mail. He also returned none of her calls.

"I think it's brilliant, dear. It's an expansion and if you work hard on this, then you'd be able to pull a lot of positive attention to the bakery this summer when we'll have a lot of tourists coming to Ivy Creek. And one thing tourists love to try out is food."

Lucy chewed on her lower lip and toyed with the pen in her hand. "I sincerely doubt Taylor would want to help. He hates me... we don't get along very well."

Tricia chuckled and took off her reading glasses as she dropped the paper she was reading. "That young man always had the hots for you. Chances are he still does."

Lucy flushed at her aunt's comment and cleared her throat.

"It seems like you're still into him, too."

"I am not," she denied quickly. "We can never get along on anything," she added, and crossed her arms over her chest.

She picked up the remote and shrugged. "Fine, if that's what you say. You'd have to ask him to put in a good word, anyway."

Tricia lifted her legs and stretched it out on the table in front of her. At fifty-two, her aunt was still very agile, and Lucy admired her strength. She was grateful she agreed to stay with her until the entire death news blew over, and her presence brought some serenity to the chaos in Lucy's life.

Tricia started channel hopping. Most of the new channels reported the same story. Dennis Fischer's death was the top headline, even though two weeks had passed since his body was found. The cops had nothing new to say about his killer besides what they already knew and shared with the public.

He died from blunt force trauma to his head, and multiple stab wounds to his chest. The murder weapon was not found, and no DNA prints besides Dennis' were found at the scene. Lucy kept up with the investigation, mainly because she could do nothing else.

Her reputation was already linked to the man's death, and everything was a mess. She didn't expect that anyone would think she was innocent, but the least the police department could do was carry out a proper investigation.

"I should go to bed," Lucy said, as she got bored with watching the same news every night.

"Goodnight," Tricia said to her as she walked into her room and shut the door. Lucy had a restless night, and the next morning, to clear her head, she went for a run.

Hannah came to work early, and they opened up the bakery, baked little quantities of pastries, and set them out before she drove out again. They went to the store to pick out items. She needed to try out a new recipe for chocolate cake. As they strolled the grocery aisles, Lucy bumped into a man while rolling her cart, and she apologized immediately.

"I'm sorry," she said. He nodded and walked past her. Lucy's gaze followed him, until Hannah finished picking out food flavors, and joined her.

"That man looks so familiar," she said, and Hannah looked at the man.

"Who?" she asked and tossed the items she held into the cart. Her gaze followed Lucy's and landed on the man looking at the shelf where stacks of whipped cream were kept. "That's Michael Trent," she said.

Lucy rolled her cart away as Hannah continued. "He runs the largest poultry farm here in Ivy Creek and supplies most of the eggs used in town."

"I've seen him somewhere. I just can't place it," Lucy murmured as she paid for her items with her credit card and Hannah helped her take them out of the store. "I think it was at the funeral," she finally said. She remembered he stood behind the crowd on the far end, and she had seen him because she was standing right next to him, too scared to let anyone in the audience know she attended the funeral.

"He was at the funeral, but he left early. I think I also bumped into him then."

She was driving down the road, heading back to the bakery, when Hannah suddenly turned towards her.

"I've heard Michael and Dennis had a long-standing feud. No one really knows what it was about, but everyone knows they weren't exactly on speaking terms. And Dennis is the only businessman, with a food-related business, who buys nothing from Michael's farm."

Lucy thought Hannah's piece of information might suggest how the people of Ivy Creek viewed the murder case. If Dennis had a long-standing feud with Michael, then why wasn't he on the suspect list? Surely the cops had to know about this and also look into Michael Trent.

Lucy's intuition told her there was more to this case, but she tried to heed Taylor's words and take her mind off it. Dennis Fischer's murder was not her problem, and she had to focus on getting her bakery more sales. This was her parent's legacy, and she couldn't let it all come to nothing.

———

Taylor was standing in front of his truck when Lucy jogged past his house that morning, and she took the chance to talk to him. He was dressed in his cop uniform, and he turned when Lucy called his name.

"Taylor," Lucy jogged to meet him, panting as she wiped her forehead with the handkerchief tucked into the pocket of her sweatpants. "I have tried to reach out to you for days now, and it's common courtesy that you return missed calls when you see them."

"Do you need something?" he asked, and Lucy nodded. His expression was blank as he waited for her to reply, and Lucy cleared her throat and stepped closer to him. His intense, dark gaze remained on her as she spoke.

"It's about putting in a good word for me with the town's council committee. I intend to apply for a permit to run a concession store by the park and…"

"Wait," he said, cutting her short. "A concession store?"

"It's a means of expansion for the bakery. A way to attract more customers to the bakery."

"I don't care what it is. You plan to run it? Is there some-thing that makes you think you'd be able to manage a concession store when you can't even get customers to the bakery?"

Lucy's breath hitched in her throat, and she flushed at his

remark. How did he know the bakery was not getting any customers?

She bit her lower lip to hide her embarrassment, and she puffed out air from her mouth, hoping it would hide the color on her cheeks. "The concession store would solve that," she replied.

"I don't have time for this," Taylor said, and took out his keys from his pocket. "Business like a concession store requires commitment. What happens when you want to leave town again? All of it would be for nothing."

"Taylor... this has nothing to do with me leaving town or what you think about me. I need your help, and I am asking for it," she pointed out. "Now, I know you might not like me much, and yes, that's on me, but Sweet Delights is my parents' legacy, and ever since Dennis' death, everything has gone south. I am trying here to hold unto the little shred of hope I have, and this... this idea I got is that shred of hope for me. So please..."

Her voice trailed off, and she closed her eyes for a moment to gather her composure. "I need this, so please think about it, and put in a good word for me if you can. I will turn in a letter of request by the end of the week, and I know when the council meets to discuss it, as Sheriff's deputy, you'll have a say. So just please, think about it."

Without another word, she turned and jogged away from him.

She spent the rest of the day worrying about her conversation with Taylor and what his response would be. She hoped he would consider helping her out.

Another day passed in the bakery with no customer, and Lucy went out later that night after her aunt had retired to bring in the chairs on the patio. A woman walked up to the bakery just as Lucy took in the last set of chairs. She was exhausted from staying the entire day working on a blog post and waiting for at least one customer to walk into the store. A man dropped by earlier and ordered a scone, but Lucy was out of scones, so he had left.

"Hi," Lucy greeted her with a smile. "Do you need something?"

"Coconut bread," she replied, but her gaze left Lucy's and traveled around the bakery.

"Come on in," Lucy said, and she allowed the lady to step in before she closed the door behind them and went to get her order. The lady smiled as she took the bag from her, and Lucy took her payment in cash.

"Have a great night," she said, but the lady didn't turn to leave.

"You cleaned up nice," she said, and Lucy dropped the bagel she had picked up. The lady looked around the place again before bringing her gaze back to Lucy.

Her green eyes held a certain interest Lucy couldn't understand. She had never met the woman before, but it was obvious she had taken a keen interest in her bakery.

"I'm sorry, have we met?"

"No, but I know something that might interest you," she replied with a smile. "I think you are innocent in the Dennis Fischer murder, and I can help you find his killer."

7

L ucy closed the doors to the bakery and pulled a chair to sit beside the lady. "I'm Grace, by the way," she said, and gave Lucy a smile.

Lucy reminded herself that she had to be cautious and not believe everything the stranger before her was about to share. Still, she couldn't deny she was interested in whatever Grace had to say.

"What I'm about to tell you might be common knowledge to you, but I am quite certain about it, and I wonder why no one else has picked up interest in it."

Lucy linked her fingers in front of her and gave Grace her full attention.

"It's about Michael Trent," she said, then sipped from her glass. "I'm sure you might have heard about his feud with Dennis."

"I might have heard a thing or two," Lucy replied, not wanting to give away any more information because she still didn't trust Grace. "Dennis made a point of not patronizing Michael's local business even though he is the largest supplier of eggs in town."

"It was more than that," Grace replied. "I worked for Michael but quit recently because I wanted to make a move into the city. I can tell you they both had frequent arguments and Michael openly made a lot of claims and threats during those arguments."

"So, you think Michael killed Dennis?" Lucy asked, and Grace shrugged.

"I'm saying it is suspicious that Dennis wound up dead in your backyard. It's more like someone is setting you up to take the fall for it."

"Have you told anyone else about this?" Lucy asked.

Grace shook her head. "It's not my business. I'm leaving town tomorrow, but I was walking by and I couldn't help but feel sorry for you. Rumors spread in Ivy Creek, and they are talking about the girl who murdered her competition."

Lucy scoffed and clenched her fists. The people in this town were more brazen than she thought. They had no evidence that she killed Dennis, but it didn't stop them from spreading the gossip. It was maddening to think that even the ones who knew her when she lived in town did nothing to defend her, even Taylor.

She remembered the cold look in his eyes when he had arrived at her bakery the morning she found the body, and how he dismissed her when she tried to talk to him after spending half of her day at the police station.

"I have to go," Grace said and pushed back in her seat. "I hope this helps."

Lucy wasn't sure if the information Grace gave her could help. She had only raised her suspicions about Michael and made it impossible for her to stay out of the situation because she was getting desperate. She needed a way out. A means to clear her name. Or else her business in Ivy Creek would be over before it even began.

"Can I contact you?" Lucy asked, and Grace nodded.

She took out a notepad, scribbled her number, then handed it over to her. "Everyone knows of Michael's feud with Dennis, but no one knows what really happened. They were once friends, and then Dennis betrayed Michael in a deal they both had. If anyone had enough reason to get back at Dennis, it's Michael. Trust me," she said with conviction.

Lucy's mind was spinning, and she tried to take her mind off the information Grace had just given her, but she couldn't. Restless, she spent the night preparing a pitch letter for the town's council board. This was her shot at turning things around for the bakery, and she had to get it right.

Lucy was exhausted the next morning, but she had promised to teach Hannah a new cake recipe, so she prepared a cup of coffee and headed down to the bakery. She put the chairs out on the patio, cleaned the tables, before getting out the ingredients needed for the day's lesson.

Lucy sat and scribbled down a list of things to do in her notepad, and she heard the door open. "Hannah, thank goodness you're here. We can get started early," she said without looking up from her notepad. "I have taken out the ingredients, so we can get started once you settle in."

Lucy expected a reply from Hannah and when she got none, she looked up to see Taylor standing by the entrance. "Hi," she said nervously, and jumped out of the chair she sat in.

"Hey," he replied, and slipped his hands into his pocket. "I thought about what you said," he began before Lucy could say anything else, and she swallowed, anticipating his reply. "It's a good idea, and I will put in a kind word for you with the board, but that is all I can do, and it guarantees nothing. It's up to you to make your pitch a persuasive one."

Lucy sighed, and a smile crept on her lips. "Thank you," she whispered.

Taylor nodded, turned around and walked out of the

bakery. Tricia came down to the bakery minutes after Taylor left, but Lucy still stood in front of her counter, speechless, and unable to gather her thoughts.

This might actually happen. I might really get committee approval, and this... this could change everything.

"I thought I heard someone."

"Yes, Taylor was here," Lucy replied, and walked over to her aunt. "He's agreed to put in a good word at the committee meeting," she squealed, and Tricia laughed.

"Oh, honey. That's amazing. I knew he would come around."

"I know," she replied breathlessly, and laughed again. "Honestly, I thought he wouldn't. He made it very clear the last time that he didn't believe I could handle running a business in town."

"Well, you've got one chance to prove him wrong," Tricia replied and gave her a soft pat on her shoulder. Lucy ran her fingers through her hair and looked around the bakery. This was a huge encouragement, and now what she needed to do was impress the board members.

———

HER IDEA of impressing the council was to throw a dinner party. Lucy and Hannah worked to get wine and food available for the dinner, while Tricia did her magic with her parents' house. Lucy sent out invitations, taking advantage of the town's ability to spread gossip, and by evening of the fixed date, her parents' living room was swamped with guests, most of whom were members of the council board.

"I have to admit Lucy, you throw one hell of a party," Luke Sanders, the leader of the committee, complimented, and Lucy smiled. She had gotten as much information as she could on them. Hannah had helped as she had been in town longer than Lucy.

"Thank you, Mr. Sanders. I'm pleased to know you're enjoying yourself," she replied.

She walked away from him to talk with her other guests, then walked into the kitchen to meet Hannah, who was shoving huge portions of apple pie in her mouth. Her pale blue shirt had streaks of pie on it, and she picked up a napkin and wiped her lips.

"You alright?" Lucy asked, and Hannah grinned.

"I'm stress eating, I know," she replied with a mouth full of pie, and Lucy laughed.

"I should be the one stress eating; I don't know how much longer I can deal with the curious but yet polite glares from these people."

Tricia entered the kitchen, adjusting the black sequin dress she wore, and she smiled at both Lucy and Hannah. "What are we doing?" she asked.

"Stress eating," Lucy replied, and took a spoonful of Hannah's apple pie. "This is really good," she moaned while complimenting the pie Hannah made. "These pies will do murder to my hips. I wonder which pie goes with murder? You're getting the hang of the recipes."

"Tricia helped," Hannah replied.

"I have to get back," Lucy said, looking at her wristwatch. She was out of the kitchen in a daze and returned to mingling with the guests.

At some point, she stood with Hannah in a corner, sipping from her glass of wine as they looked around with a satisfied smile.

"You think this will butter them up?" Hannah asked, but Lucy's gaze had wandered to Michael. She watched him, and Grace's words flashed in her head. *If anyone has a reason to hurt Dennis, then it's Michael. Trust me.*

"Lucy?" Hannah said and followed her gaze. Lucy blinked and turned to her. "What's the deal with Michael?"

"Nothing," she replied and looked at him again. He turned, and his gaze met with hers from where he stood. Lucy's breath hitched in her throat, and she looked away immediately.

"It's not nothing. You keep staring at him," Hannah said and then frowned. "I also think it is strange that he's chatting with Mrs. Fischer, but you don't see me gawking at him."

"Don't you think it's weird?" Lucy asked, and the frown on Hannah's face deepened. "I mean Michael, and Dennis weren't exactly close, and now Dennis, her husband is dead. It's like she is fraternizing with the enemy."

"We don't know that he's the enemy," Hannah cut in, and Lucy sighed. She turned to Hannah, took her arm, and pulled her into the kitchen.

"I think Michael had something to do with it," she said in a hushed tone. "With Dennis' murder, I mean think about it. He has a long-standing feud with the man. Everyone in town knows this, and by all accounts, they've had several altercations, and Michael threw threats around. Does that not strike you as suspicious?"

"Yes, but… there's no proof that he did it."

"I know, that's why I have to find out what happened."

"You mean, you'll let the cops do their job, right?" Hannah interrupted, and Lucy straightened her posture. She had thought about what Grace said to her and the fact was she couldn't sit back and do nothing.

"The future of my bakery depends on clearing my reputation in this town, and I don't see any cops lining up to do that," she said.

Hannah sighed, then folded her arms over her chest. "What do you need me to do?" she asked.

Lucy smiled. "Entertain the guests and leave the rest to me."

She walked out of the kitchen with Hannah and noticed that Michael was gone. Lucy sucked in a deep breath and decided to speak with Dennis' wife. Sophie Fischer wasn't exactly the kind of woman she would expect to live with a man like Dennis. Unlike her husband, she seemed pleasant and gentle.

There was a warm smile on Sophie's face when Lucy walked up to her and extended a hand. "Lucy Hale," she introduced as they shook hands.

"You've thrown an amazing house party, Lucy," Sophie complimented, and Lucy fixed her gaze on her green eyes. "It's refreshing to have someone young around trying hard to keep the old ones happy."

"It's really nothing," Lucy replied. "My parents threw dinner parties like this all the time."

Sophie nodded and dropped the glass she held onto a tray that a server passing by held. Lucy watched her snuggle under the shawl wrapped around her shoulders.

"I'm really sorry about your husband, and I had nothing to do with it," she said apologetically, and saw Sophie's gaze turn cold. A chill spread through her arms, and she swallowed. "I just wanted you to know how sorry I am," she stammered.

"This must be inconvenient for you, the rumors about my husband, and..." Sophie's voice trailed off, but she continued, maintaining the smile on her face even though her gaze remained icy. "I am really sorry, that you have to take all the snide remarks and innuendo about his murder, dear."

Lucy didn't think a person could maintain a distinct proportion of two emotions at once, but Sophie's gaze sent shivers down her spine even though her smile remained warm. "Throwing a good party to butter up the committee members. Are you trying to expand? So, you want to get a permit?"

"Mrs. Fischer..."

"Sophie," she interrupted, and just then Lucy saw Michael walk towards them. "You bake a decent apple and pecan pie, so I'm sure you'll excel if you expand," she continued.

She expected the woman to curse her, considering the rumors around town, but Sophie's reaction was totally unexpected.

"I wish you well," she added when Michael reached where they stood and placed his hand on her shoulder.

"You ready?" Michael asked and flashed a smile in Lucy's direction. Sophie nodded and walked away with him.

Hannah walked over to Lucy minutes later and asked. "How did that go?"

"Unexpectedly, well," she replied, and her gaze remained on Michael and Sophie until they were out of sight.

Later that night, Lucy received a reply on her application to the committee.

8

"It wasn't really a no," Hannah said, trying to be encouraging after Lucy showed her the email she received from the board the previous night.

"It's a sugar-coated no," Tricia cut in from where she sat at the counter, nursing a cup of heavy-creamed coffee. Lucy buried her face in her hands and closed her eyes. "These people are so polite; they wouldn't tell you no in plain terms. They'd dance around it for as long as they want when in reality all they're really saying is no."

"They say your application is open to consideration. It means they could deliberate on it later on and change their minds," Hannah said.

"Are you sure Taylor put in a good word? Maybe we should..." Tricia said.

"I don't want to hear it, aunt," Lucy cut in gently. "I'm not asking Taylor for help again. This is already as humiliating as it can get," she added with a defeated sigh.

"Let's focus on running this bakery in the meantime," Hannah suggested. "We got two customers yesterday, and hopefully we'll get some more today," she said in a high-pitched tone.

Lucy smiled at her, grateful for her support, and glanced at her watch. "It's six pm. I don't think we'll get another customer, unless it's someone returning something they ordered," she said.

Tricia exhaled and walked over to where Hannah and Lucy sat. "I mean, dear, your pie is the best I've tasted in a long time. It's a refreshing blend of flavors and it has a rich, buttery taste. Only a person with no taste buds would say otherwise."

"Thanks, aunt," Lucy whispered as Tricia squeezed her shoulder.

Lucy loved how her aunt had a distinct way of encouraging her, and the humor she attached to everything always made being around her fun. Growing up, Tricia was her favorite relative, and whenever her parents needed time out from parenting, they dropped her for the weekend at Stone Creek, a town a few miles from Ivy Creek where Tricia lived. Those weekends were always spent in parks, swimming pools, and shopping malls, and Lucy had bonded with her aunt that way.

"Now, wipe that sullen look off your pretty face, dear, and go out and have some fun. Hannah and I will clean up here," she said, and Lucy looked at Hannah, who nodded at her.

She didn't feel like going out, but maybe a walk would clear her head. She passed the high road and entered an adjoining street leading to the town's library, when an art store caught her attention.

Lucy crossed the road and walked into the store to look. She went through the displayed paintings and then spotted a mural with bright, vibrant colors. Lucy stood, admiring the painting. It was a lovely, expressive piece, and as she stared at it, she tried to imagine it on a corner of her bakery's wall.

"It's a lovely piece of art," a female voice said behind her, and Lucy turned around to find a beautiful brunette smiling at her.

"Diane Keen," she said and extended her hand. Lucy smiled and accepted the gesture.

"Lucy Hale," she replied.

"Oh, I know you," Diane said. "The entire town's been buzzing with rumors about you for weeks."

Lucy felt heat rise to the back of her neck. *Did every person in this town know her as a murder suspect? Was Dennis' death the only thing they talked about in their spare time?*

"I'm sorry if I made you feel uncomfortable," Diane added immediately, and Lucy waved her hand dismissively. Diane was oddly familiar to her, but she couldn't place the face yet.

"It's not a big deal," Lucy replied. "It's a small town. People talk."

"They do," Diane agreed and then focused on the mural again. "I just hope the news blows over soon," she continued. "It's horrific what happened to Dennis," she paused. "And to you, of course. No one should be accused of such a terrible crime."

Lucy wished she would drop the subject, so she casually asked. "How much does this cost?"

"I have to check on that," Diane replied with a smile. "I'm new around here, and I'm not yet familiar with the price of these pieces," she added with a laugh. "It's not been an easy transition from being a chef to an art sales rep."

Lucy followed her as she walked over to the counter to check her system for the price of the mural, and she asked. "You were a chef?"

"Yes, I worked for Dennis," she replied without looking up from her screen. "Three years I slaved for him and helped expand his business. And the jerk pays me back by firing me for no just cause," she said when she looked up.

"Oh," Lucy exclaimed. *Just how many enemies did Dennis have?*

"Forty bucks," Diane said and Lucy blinked. "For the mural."

Lucy reached into her satchel purse hanging on her shoulder and handed over a fifty-dollar bill. It was a cheap artwork to add to the decorations in the bakery. "So, why did Dennis fire you?" she asked casually as Diane issued a receipt.

"I have no idea," she replied. "All I know is one morning I'm baking, and the next minute he's asking to speak with me privately. Turns out his crazy wife somehow convinced him to let some staff go because they were facing some financial hardship, and I was one of the workers to take the hit."

"Crazy wife?" Lucy asked and took the receipt handed over to her. Diane took a box and packaged the sixteen square feet mural painting.

"Yes, everyone in town knows she's got dementia. Dennis had her checked into a mental home out of town for some time, and later brought her back home when it seemed like she got better. But it turns out she wasn't better.

"I just want to put the entire ordeal behind me, and I needed a new job to get by, so I took the first thing I could get. Although it hurt me deeply that he could discard one of his workers without a second thought."

Lucy took the box from her and smiled. "Thanks," she said, then turned and walked out of the store. On her way back home, she decided to make a quick stop at Taylor's house and hoped he would listen to what she had to say.

She met his mother. Mrs. Baker was pleased to see Lucy had dropped by, and she offered her a glass of water while they talked about Lucy's bakery. Lucy was shocked to see his mother as she knew Taylor lived on his own, but she engaged in the conversation until Taylor walked in and his surprise to see her in his house was evident in the look he gave her.

"Do you have a minute?" Lucy asked when his mother excused them, and Taylor came to sit on the couch opposite her. "I got a reply from the committee," she began. "They refused my proposal."

"I'm sorry," he replied, his gaze not leaving hers, and she shrugged and forced a smile.

"That's not why I'm here though," she said and adjusted on her seat. "Is there any update on the investigation?"

"I'm not at liberty to tell you anything about the investigation, Lucy," he replied.

"I know that, but... I just need to know that you're one step closer to finding the culprit and this entire ordeal will be behind me soon."

"I'm not at liberty to say," he replied and stood up. "It's best you find something else to keep you busy," he said and moved to walk past her, but her next words stopped him.

"Did you know about Michael's feud with Dennis? And that he was going bankrupt?"

Taylor sighed as he turned to her, and she rose from where she sat. Lucy raised her chin when he fixed his gaze on hers, and she added. "I found out from a chef he recently fired before he died, and she had a lot to say about his wife."

"Did you go around asking questions about Dennis' murder?"

"No, but..."

"Good, you shouldn't do that," he warned. "If you're not his killer, then that means his killer is still out there. So, what do you think happens when you dig into matters that do not concern you?"

"I'm trying to clear my name here. I don't see you or any other cop in line to help me do that."

"Just let us do our job please, and focus on running your

bakery," he replied. "Murder cases are not the same as stories you upload on your blog, and it takes a lot of work to catch a killer. If you go about digging, you'll either get the killer on your tail or you'll wind up dead."

His gaze softened on hers a little, and he added. "It's not safe." Lucy retreated and walked out of his house.

Lucy spent most of the night staring at the mural and replaying the chef's words in her head. Something told her there was more to the story, and she could find out more if she followed the chef around a little. Something about Diane's story piqued her curiosity, and she couldn't push down the thoughts racing through her mind. She dozed off late and awoke to the sound of a loud crash from her bakery downstairs.

9

_T_ricia had her arms around Lucy, and they watched as the cops hauled a teenage boy away the next morning. Lucy cleared her throat when Taylor walked over to where she stood with her aunt and tried to act like she wasn't freaked out. The cops had asked around, and the eyewitness descriptions of some passersby matched the boy's physical description.

"That's him?" she asked, and Taylor nodded. "A teenage boy threw some stones at my window for no reason?"

"He will give his statement to the cops. For now, what we know is that someone paid him to do so. All he said was they wanted to send you a message."

"A message?"

"Have you been digging around Dennis' murder when I asked you to sit back?"

Lucy shrugged. "I spoke with you last night. How much digging do you think I would have done in a few hours?"

Taylor sighed, then placed his hands on his hips, and turned to watch the cop's car drive away. Lucy kept her gaze focused on the road. "This is not what I expected when I decided to stay in town," she murmured beneath her breath, and Tricia, who was beside her, gently patted her shoulder.

"I will keep you posted," Taylor said, then walked away, leaving Lucy and her aunt to clean up the mess.

When she had heard the first crash, she had jumped out of her bed and rushed to her window to check out what was happening. By the time she got downstairs, there was no one outside, and three of her windows were broken.

"I don't understand any of this," Lucy lamented as Tricia helped her take out the broken shards of glass. The repairs would cost her a lot of money and she wasn't even making any profit from the bakery to justify the capital she had put into running it.

"Do you think there is a reason for anyone to target you?" Tricia asked.

"I have no idea," she replied and wrapped her arms around her chest. "They all think I killed Dennis anyway, so I don't know what's going on."

Tricia scrunched her nose. "I'll tell you what, we'll get to the bottom of this together," she said and stepped outside to throw most of the pieces of glass in the waste bin. When she returned, she handed over an envelope to Lucy.

"I think someone dropped this," she said. "Found it lying around on the patio."

Lucy took the envelope and opened it, and color drained from her face. "No, they didn't just leave it lying around," Lucy replied as her eyes scanned the two words written boldly in red on the piece of paper inside the envelope.

It read, *STOP DIGGING.*

Tricia took the paper out of her hands and read it out loud. Her aunt's face paled, and Lucy dropped to a chair so she wouldn't lose her balance. "This has to do with Dennis' murder," she whispered and her thoughts whirled around everything she had uncovered just by asking questions.

Dennis had fired his chef unjustly, and he also had a long-standing feud with Michael Trent. To Lucy, those were two suspects in the murder, and she still couldn't figure out what Taylor was doing about it.

"I met someone," Lucy said to her aunt. "She used to work with Dennis, but he fired her before he was killed. She had some interesting things to say about Dennis Fischer."

"What did she tell you?" Tricia asked and took a seat in front of Lucy.

"Dennis was bankrupt."

Tricia's eyes widened, and Lucy nodded. "That was my exact reaction because this man flaunted cash at me to get me to sell Sweet Delights."

"Who else have you talked to about this?"

"Taylor… he is the sheriff's deputy, and he said he would look into it," Lucy replied, and shook her head. "But I'm done being the obedient girl while this town sucks the life out of everything I'm working so hard for. I have to look into this myself, and I need your help."

"Where do we start?" Tricia asked, her eyes gleaming with mischief, and Lucy's brilliant idea was to pay the chef another visit.

———

LUCY DROVE out with her aunt to the high street and parked at a corner of the street where they could look into the art shop. Her eyes widened in surprise when she saw Diane talking with Michael.

Seeing Diane and Michael together put her on edge, and she suspected she was the center of their discussion. Everyone in town seemed to be talking about her. Every inch of her wanted to know what their discussion was about, and she could see from her aunt's focused look that she shared the same view.

"When I spoke to Diane, she mentioned nothing about being close with Michael," Lucy murmured as she watched them hug before Michael walked away from the store, and Diane went back inside.

"Should we go in?" Tricia asked, and Lucy shook her head.

"Let's watch from a distance," she suggested, and popped a stick of gum in her mouth. Tricia's keen gaze remained fixed on the entrance to the art store, and Lucy took out her phone and checked the time.

She yawned, closed her eyes for a minute. She startled when she felt a double pat on her arm.

"She's leaving," Tricia announced in an excited voice, and Lucy looked.

They watched Diane close the door to the art store, then flag down a cab. Lucy started the engine of her car and drove down the road behind the cab.

They drove a while and stopped at the town's clinic.

"Is she ill?" Tricia asked and Lucy shrugged.

"I think you should wait here," she told her aunt, then took off her seatbelt and got out of the car before Tricia could suggest anything else. She walked into the clinic while adjusting the black cap on her head and took the seat at the corner of the reception area.

Diane stood at the counter, and Lucy watched the woman standing on the other end give her directions. She waited, watching closely as Diane smiled and thanked the lady before following the directions.

Lucy sprang into action. She followed her down the corridor, careful not to gain her attention, and stopped when Diane knocked on a door, and walked into a room with the sign, OB-GYN.

Lucy did a double take. *Was Diane pregnant?*

Was Michael the father? Both of them had seemed quite close. Maybe they had such a relationship?

She didn't know what to think, but this was a positive step towards finding out more about what was going on in Ivy Creek. She had a strong feeling of Michael's involvement, and now all she had to do was find some evidence to back it up.

Lucy returned to the car.

"What did you see?" Tricia asked the moment she got in.

"She went in to see an Obstetrician, I think she's pregnant."

Tricia gasped. "You think it's Michael's?"

"I don't know what to think," Lucy replied as they drove back to the bakery to meet Hannah. "I think we have to find out what Michael is up to ourselves, and it will involve following him around."

"I have a better idea," Tricia said later that evening when they had closed up for the day. Lucy was in the middle of fixing dinner, and she listened to her aunt.

"We get into his house and search."

"That's a crime," Lucy pointed out, and Tricia shrugged.

"Not if we don't get caught," she replied, a wide grin on her face that made Lucy laugh and shake her head.

"This is fun for you?"

"Come on, you have to admit it's thrilling... We're like private detectives, and watching that chef today made me realize we might actually be good at this."

Lucy smiled and shook her head. She needed little convincing. They watched Michael for a few days and monitored his every move. He lived alone in a house close to the entrance of his farm and drove a white truck.

It was the biggest farm in town, but what caught Lucy's attention was the fact that he had no workers living on the

RUTH BAKER

farm with him. The perfect opportunity presented itself when Michael drove out one Sunday evening to take supplies to the local market.

Lucy watched him drive out in his truck with the back fully loaded, and once he was out of sight, she got out of her car parked close by, then approached the farm house with her aunt. She hoped they would find at least one clue that would help with the puzzle.

After crawling through an unopened window, they found nothing linking Michael to Dennis. The man had a simple house, and most of his belongings were personal. Lucy found pictures on the wall of him and a little girl. He had no wife, no children, and she thought it was a sad life. They ended the search early because of the fear of getting caught.

"I still think if we keep digging, we could find something," Tricia said one evening as they watched the local news.

It was the middle of summer, and many tourists were in town. It made visiting the parks or hike grounds tedious because there were many people in line.

Lucy preferred to stay indoors at times like this. When her parents were alive, the bakery would have had a lot of customers strolling in, wanting to taste her mother's famous lemon meringue pie.

Feeling nostalgic, she had baked the pie herself, copying the entire recipe she had learned as a girl, and it tasted perfect. Lucy gave Hannah the day off because she had been working diligently, opening the bakery early, setting up only a quarter portion of all the snacks they had on the menu. They hardly had any customers and staying the entire day doing nothing wasn't fair to Hannah.

"I was very positive when I started this out," Lucy said in a low voice, and took the last bit of pie. "I said to myself… you can do this, Lucy," she added, groaned and dropped her plate. "Mom would be so disappointed."

"Don't say that," Tricia cut in. "There is nothing to be disappointed about. Every failure is a stepping stone to success."

"Well, I don't even have time to fail," she replied with a huff, and waved her hand. "Look around... this place is deserted. No one drops by, and even when one person does, they seem more interested in wanting to know where or how I found the body. It's all they want to know."

"It's a rumor that will fade, Lucy. When I was eighteen, I went for a frat party and got arrested and no one in town would shut up about it for months. Eventually they got over it and found some more juicy story to talk about. The same will happen with Dennis... they'll catch the killer, and soon no one will remember any of it."

Lucy ran her fingers through her hair and stared at the painting she had gotten hanging on the wall. *How long was soon going to take?*

"I don't know how much longer I can hang onto a tiny shred of hope," she murmured. "Maybe Taylor was right... This town is not for me," she added, then stood up and headed to her apartment upstairs.

1 0

$\mathcal{L}$ucy was showing Hannah some icing techniques when someone walked into the bakery. She wiped the icing sugar off her hands, then went out to check on the customer, but gasped when she saw Sophie standing by the counter.

Lucy forced a smile as Sophie smiled at her.

"I love what you've done with this place," Sophie said. "And that mural hanging over there is lovely. Did you make it?"

"No, got it at a local store," Lucy replied casually, and Sophie smiled. "Do you need something?"

"I'm leaving town," she announced, and smiled. "I know... I just walk in here and tell you I'm leaving town for no reason," she continued, and Lucy could only blink. "But it's been a thought process for now, and it's best I leave."

"What? Why?" Lucy asked, not understanding what angle Sophie was coming from, or why she was even here telling her this. "What about Springs' bakery? I mean, you own the place now, right?"

"I completed a deal and sold out. It was something Dennis

64

and I wanted to do for a long time, but we both didn't see any of this coming," she continued, and her eyes watered. Lucy watched as Sophie tried to control her confused expression. She exhaled and closed her eyes for a moment. When she opened them again, she looked calmer, more in control as she added. "I hear the rumors in town, and I know how difficult it must be for you, trying to fit in here when everyone thinks the worse of you."

Yeah, you have no idea.

"I'm trying my best," she replied instead of the words that flashed through her head, and Sophie nodded.

"I know. That is why I completed the deal to sell the place. My husband wanted all of this, but I didn't. Now that it's done, you're the only bakery available to the locals, and they will have no choice but to patronize you."

Lucy didn't know if to feel grateful for the thoughtful gesture or angry that Sophie would think she desperately needed to make sales. "Either way, I just wanted to stop by here and let you know that."

"Is there any specific reason you've decided to sell?" Lucy asked, but Sophie shook her head. "I met with Diane Keen, a friend of your husband's," she continued, and saw the vein in Sophie's temple pulse and her eyes bulge.

"Employee," she replied. "Diane Keen was his employee, not a friend."

"Right... she told me she was unjustly fired, and I just thought that maybe your selling out was a result of internal staff issues you couldn't manage?"

Sophie shook her head. "It was the right call to sell out," she replied, and adjusted her purse beneath her arm. "Diane Keen was fired because she wasn't useful to the bakery anymore."

"Alright," Lucy said and raised her hand. She had

mentioned Diane specifically because Diane stated Sophie was behind her losing her job.

Sophie nodded. "I should get going," she said and as she turned away, Lucy noticed she was reluctant to leave. She waited until Sophie walked out of the bakery, and then she returned to the kitchen to join Hannah.

"That took a long time," Hannah said, and she nodded.

"That was Sophie Fischer," she announced.

"What did she want? Pie? Tacos?"

"She's closing up Springs' bakery, said it was the right call."

Hannah stopped piping designs unto the cake and looked at Lucy. "That's strange."

"I think so, too," she replied, then continued with her work, but she couldn't get her mind to stop spinning with thoughts of how Diane and Michael were possibly linked to Dennis' death. Lucy made time that evening to visit the art store with Tricia.

They watched from a distance as Diane closed up the art store, and they tailed her down the street. Her house was a few blocks from the art store, and Lucy parked her car by the corner of the street, then followed Diane towards the entrance of the building.

She planned to follow her and find out where she lived, so she could come back with Tricia some other time to search the house. While she loitered around in reception as Diane talked to a man by the security post, she didn't notice when Diane slipped away.

Lucy groaned and rushed towards the elevator, hoping she could meet up with her, but it was too late. She couldn't find Diane anywhere.

The next evening as Lucy sipped a cup of coffee, she wondered how she could have let Diane slip out of her gaze.

She was determined to be more vigilant, as she couldn't afford any more blunders.

She left Tricia and Hannah at the bakery and followed the woman everywhere. Diane met with Michael every evening. He walked her to her apartment down the street, but Lucy never followed her inside when Michael was around. She didn't know how dangerous he was, and it was best she avoided running into him for now.

She got another chance to find out her apartment number one evening after Diane closed the art store, and she took it.

Lucy followed her into the elevator, but she kept the black hoodie she wore over her head, and dark shades over her eyes so Diane wouldn't recognize her. They had met only once, but she suspected the woman would find her familiar.

The elevator door opened, and Lucy hesitated, giving Diane room to get out first before she followed. They walked down the corridor, and when Diane turned around, she turned to a door by her left, and pretended to unlock it until Diane stopped in front of her apartment door, then slipped into it.

Lucy sighed, and rushed to the door she saw Diane enter, and made a mental note of the apartment number. "207," she muttered, then turned to walk away, but the door opened suddenly, and someone grabbed her arm.

Lucy yelped as Diane dragged her into the apartment, shut the door, then pushed the hoodie off her head. "Are you following me?" Diane shrieked and stepped away from her. She saw recognition flash in Diane's eyes, and she sighed.

"Yes," she admitted.

"All week? What are you… a stalker?"

"No, not all week, but a few days," she replied quickly, but Diane shook her head and reached into her pocket.

"I'm calling the cops."

Lucy raised a brow. "Really? You want to call the cops when you are hiding something yourself?"

"What are you talking about?"

Lucy rolled her eyes. "Dennis Fischer's murder? And your secret pregnancy, and meetings with Michael Trent?"

Diane shrieked again, and her eyes widened. "You think I killed Dennis?"

Lucy crossed her arms over her chest as Diane scoffed. "Well, you have good reason to," she replied.

"I'm not a psychopath. I wouldn't kill someone who fired me unjustly. Suing them would work much better."

"Then why didn't you?"

Diane rolled her eyes at Lucy, then pushed her hair away from her face. "You had every right to sue him, but you didn't. Looks to me like you took matters into your hands, or asked Michael for help. You two seem really close."

"I didn't kill Dennis, that's the truth. His death was as shocking to me as it was to you," she said, and her voice trailed off. "I would never do that to the father of my child."

Shocked, Lucy stammered. "Dennis is the father?"

"We had an affair," Diane admitted. "For years he told me he loved me and he made me believe he would leave his wife for me, but he never did that. Whenever I brought it up, he always got out of the argument by saying his wife was sick and it wasn't the right time. I found out I was pregnant a few weeks before he fired me," she continued and crossed her arms over her chest. "The bakery was running at a loss. Had been for months because Dennis was deceived into purchasing a fake property and he was laying off workers, so he saw it as a perfect opportunity to get rid of me. He offered me cash to get rid of the baby, and then he turned up dead the next day. I have no idea what happened to him… that's the truth."

Lucy blinked and looked away from her. *Could she believe*

what Diane was saying? She had figured the part about the pregnancy, but she would never have guessed that the child was for Dennis. Did Sophie know about this too? Was that why she was so tense when Diane's name came up?

"I didn't kill Dennis, but I can't say the same for Michael," Diane suddenly said, and Lucy lifted her gaze to hers again. She saw the scared look in the woman's eyes as she added. "Michael and I have been close friends a long time, and the night I told him about the pregnancy, I had never seen him more enraged."

———

LUCY TOLD Tricia everything Diane said to her. "Dennis is more of a jerk than we all thought he was," Tricia said when she finished her story, and she nodded. "I think Michael did it."

"Me, too," Lucy admitted. "He has more than one reason to want him dead, and he's never hidden his dislike for Dennis because everyone in town knows."

"We have to find proof."

Lucy was chopping vegetables and tossing them into a bowl of water. She prepared a kale salad for lunch and spent the time with her aunt plotting another visit to Michael's farm.

It was a cool Sunday evening, and he would be driving out to make supplies any minute, so all they needed to do was get ready. They snuck into Michael's house through the kitchen window. Lucy knew this wasn't the best approach to solving Dennis murder. Breaking into Michael's house was a criminal offense, and if she got caught then she'd be in so much trouble, but she couldn't think of any other means.

The end has to justify the means, she thought to herself when they got into the house.

Tricia searched his living room, and Lucy found a door in the corridor that led to the basement. She called her aunt, and together they went into the basement. It was dark and dusty down there.

"I don't think there will be much to find here," Tricia said as Lucy mistakenly knocked over a flower vase on the table and it crashed to the ground. They both froze, and looked around, trying to make out objects with the flashlight Lucy held tightly in one hand.

Tricia sneezed and took out a handkerchief from her pocket. They walked over to the shelf hanging on the wall, and Lucy looked at the stack of papers, then pulled out one.

She opened it and flipped through the pages.

"What did you find?" Tricia asked.

"A ledger," she replied as her gaze narrowed down on the notes scribbled on different pages. She used her phone to take pictures of the pages so she could go through them later, then she dropped the paper and took out another.

"This is a cute picture," Tricia said and Lucy walked over to look at it. "Isn't that…"

"It's Sophie," Lucy interrupted as she stared at the picture of Michael and Sophie, with his arms around her neck and his lips on her cheeks. They both looked happy in the picture, and Lucy cleared her throat. "I don't think anyone is supposed to see this."

Tricia took out her phone and took a picture. "I will send it to you, it might come in handy."

Lucy nodded. "This might mean Sophie had a relationship with Michael, and this is one more reason why he would want Dennis out of the picture."

"There's more," Tricia announced, and took out a small album. She flipped through the pictures, most of Michael alone, and others with Sophie. Lucy looked around some more and saw a baseball bat on the floor beside a soccer cleats.

"Let's get out of here," she said when she found nothing else of importance, and Tricia dropped the album. As they made it out of the basement, they both heard the loud sound of cop sirens close by and knew that this time there was no way out.

"I told you to stay out of it," Taylor chided, pacing around his office while Lucy sat with her head bowed. "You don't listen... you never listen," he continued. "You broke into a man's house. That is a chargeable crime, and you could get a year for that."

Lucy closed her eyes as he continued to rant. *This is so embarrassing,* she thought. Michael had returned early from his trip into town and realized someone had broken into his house when he found the door to the basement ajar. They had been lost in their search and lost track of time, and Michael had used that opportunity to call the cops.

"Taylor..."

"You don't seem to get it, do you? You go about causing a scene, not caring about what it would take others to get you out of the mess you put yourself in. You're no different from the spoiled brat you were five years ago when you left town."

"Is this about me leaving town? Or about Michael's house?" she retorted and raised her head. "I don't see you or anyone else doing anything to get this murder solved," she said.

"Do not accuse me of not doing my job, Lucy."

"Why? I found out Dennis had a secret affair with his chef. I got the chef to point me in the right direction, and I got to find out Michael has a thing for Sophie."

"If you stayed out of it, then I wouldn't have to be here, saving you, again," he threw back at her. "Can you not cause any more trouble?" he asked and shoved his hands through his hair. He squeezed his eyes shut, and she noticed the fine lines around the corners of his eyes.

"I had to do something," she muttered. Lucy had mixed emotions about the situations she found herself in. She was one step closer to finding out the truth, and that was what mattered to her, not what Taylor thought of her.

"I'm not backing down now," she said in a quiet tone, and stood up. "You either have to charge me for this crime or let me get back to work."

Taylor turned to face her again. His cheeks reddened, and Lucy raised her chin defiantly, preparing herself for whatever he was about to say next. *I can handle whatever he throws at me.*

He gritted his teeth. "Just do as you're told and stay out of this because I won't let you go free the next time you break the law."

Taylor left his office, and Lucy walked out after him minutes later. "God, I can't stand him," she told her aunt as they walked out of the station, and Tricia laughed.

"Did they charge you?"

She shook her head. "I will have to pay a fine, but I think that's it."

As they got outside, Lucy saw Sophie and Michael get out of a car and walk towards the station. "I overheard the cops talking," Tricia said. "They are here for questioning."

"Why would they come in together?" Lucy asked.

"They are each other's alibi," Tricia replied. "I heard they were together the night Dennis was murdered, so their whereabouts sync. And it takes them off the suspect list."

Lucy shook her head as they flagged down a cab to take them back home. "They are no longer hiding their affair. Maybe this means they murdered him together... I mean, what better way to have Sophie all to himself, than get rid of her husband who was sleeping around himself?"

———

LUCY WENT for a run early the next morning. It was a good way to start her day. When she stepped out of the building, she saw Michael's truck parked in a corner of the road. He started the engine the minute she spotted him, and sped down the road, leaving a trail of dust behind him, and Lucy turned white with fear.

She focused on her path and completed her jog in thirty minutes, and by the time she returned to the bakery, Hannah was already setting up the patio. Her schedule for the day got less vigorous with each passing day, and recently they barely baked anything for sale because no one came by.

Lucy focused on running her blog and making more posts. A few emails came in from her publishing house, and she had been tempted to reply and tell them she was coming back to town, but what stopped her was the thought of leaving the bakery and everything she grew up with.

Since her parents died, she had been feeling nostalgic, and the urge to fit back into life here was growing. Lucy wanted to focus on something bigger than herself. She had her blog, and even though it was running smoothly, it didn't seem enough.

Running the bakery was an achievement she would have loved to add to the list, and proof to herself that she could handle anything. But so far, all she could prove was that the town she felt so attached to, had changed so much in her absence. And there was nothing she could do about it.

Lucy drove to the park and dropped by Big Joe's stand. She spent time walking in the park and finally sat down to watch the children playing. From where she sat, she spotted a cop playing with his child on the field, and the mother standing by a corner watching, and the image made her laugh.

She remembered taking walks with Taylor some years back. They joked about everything they saw and admired watching families having fun. Back then, she had imagined a life in Ivy Creek; setting up a family, running a business, and being content. But a big opportunity had come, and she changed her plans.

For the first time, Lucy wondered how things would have been different if she had stayed. She would have earned the respect of Ivy Creek and they wouldn't all see her as the spoiled brat who ran and abandoned everyone.

Maybe Taylor was right, and she shouldn't have tried to run the bakery at all. Things wouldn't have been so messy if she had just taken Dennis' offer.

It was late when Lucy finally got back in her car to drive back home. As she made it down the high road, a van came out of the adjoining road and sped in her direction. Lucy stepped on her brakes, but the car didn't slow down. She swerved, trying to dodge the oncoming van, but couldn't control her speed.

She crashed into a fire hydrant at the corner of the road. Her head lolled forward and collided with the air bag that popped out of the steering wheel.

———

THE NEXT TIME she opened her eyes, the pain that shot through her head was unbearable, and all she could hear were murmurs. Lucy swallowed, and blinked. Then slowly the murmurs made sense as she saw Hannah and Tricia peering down at her with worry written all over their faces.

"Are you alright? You were hurt," her aunt said as she swallowed again and tried to speak.

"What happened?" She asked as she touched her head and felt the bandage wrapped around it.

"You were in an accident," Hannah replied. "The cops are here to ask what happened."

Lucy cleared her throat when a cop walked into the room alongside Taylor, and her aunt walked out with Hannah.

"How are you feeling?" The officer asked and she nodded gently. "Can you tell us what happened?"

"A truck…" she stammered, then cleared her throat again. Her gaze landed on Taylor's and for a moment, there seemed to be a flicker of concern in his eyes. It disappeared as quickly as it came, and he focused on his partner. "It came out of nowhere, and I tried to slow down, but I couldn't... The brakes…"

"The brakes didn't work?" Taylor asked, and she nodded.

"Have you had issue with your brakes in the past few weeks or months?"

"No," she replied. "Its been fine."

"Do you think someone tampered with them?" The other cop asked Taylor, and just then she remembered seeing Michael by her bakery that same day. *What if he had tried to hurt her, and tampered with her brakes?*

She swallowed again. "Michael," she said. "I saw him loitering around my bakery earlier before the accident happened. You think it's related?"

The cop was about to reply, but Taylor cut in. "Don't assume anything… we'll look into it carefully," he said, then walked out of the room. Tricia and Hannah entered again, and Lucy sighed.

"You would think Taylor would show a little compassion or pretend to like me when I'm hurt, but he's plain cold."

"The man has never been a pretender," Tricia replied, and that was true. In the years Lucy had known him, he was pretty easy to read, and she could instantly tell when he was offended or happy.

How had the years changed him? They used to be such good friends who enjoyed each other's company so much, but leaving town had changed that. It had changed him just as much as it changed her.

Lucy was discharged the next morning after the doctors ran a routine scan to make sure she had no internal injuries, and she spent the rest of the day resting in her room. When she finally got down to the bakery, Hannah offered her a piece of cake. Lucy sat back and enjoyed the thick cinnamon filling that gave it a rich taste.

"Did you hear?" Tricia asked as she entered the bakery holding shopping bags. Both Lucy and Hannah chorused.

"Hear what?"

"They arrested Michael Trent this morning after the cops searched his house and found brake parts of a car in his basement."

Lucy was not shocked by the news. Her intuition had told her Michael had something to do with it. It was payback for breaking into his house, or a way to scare her off from digging into Dennis' death. Either way, he was wrong, and all of this only made her more desperate to know what really happened the night Dennis died.

1 2

---

*H*er intuition turned out to be wrong. Lucy was lost in reading through the ledger pictures on her phone when someone barged into the bakery. She looked up from her laptop and saw Michael storming towards her, his face red and the veins on his temple pulsing.

"You should be in jail," she said and rushed out of her chair, backing away from him as he came closer. "Come any closer and I'm calling the cops," she threatened and raised her cell phone so he could see she wasn't joking.

"Turns out they have no reason to charge me," Michael snapped, and she shook her head.

"Why?" *do I need to give the cops evidence myself?* "You tampered with my brakes; they found the brakes in your house... The basement."

"Those belonged to my car," he pointed out. "I came to warn you to get off my back. I have nothing to do with whatever mess you're in, and I don't care what you are doing. Just stop dragging me into this mess."

"Oh, come on. Cut the crap," Lucy replied and pushed

back a stray strand of hair from her face. "We both know you're not innocent. Not while you're sneaking around with Dennis's wife everywhere in town. Does she know? Does she know you killed him? Or did you both plan it together?"

"I didn't kill Dennis," he said, and Lucy raised her eyebrow. "Look, I don't have to defend myself to you, or anyone else. I told the cops everything I know, and I don't have to defend your baseless accusations. I'm sorry you got hurt, but that wasn't me."

"I read your ledgers… Dennis tricked you on a business deal and walked away with all the profit. You hated him, and all the while you were having an affair with his wife."

"I'm not in a relationship with Sophie," he interrupted, then burst into laughter. "You think I'm having an affair with her? She's a friend, a close friend and she came to me when she found out her husband was having an affair. All I've done is to support a friend and make sure she's getting by because even after Dennis did that to her, she still loved him. I always told her he was a jerk, but she wouldn't listen. Diane is also a friend and I have to admit, it annoyed me that Dennis toyed with and hurt two women close to my heart, but I sure as hell didn't kill him."

Lucy flushed in embarrassment when Michael revealed he was just friends with Sophie. "If you think I'm lying, then ask the cops. We've given our statements together from the very start of this, and everything you think you know; they know too."

Lucy turned away from him for a moment. When she turned back, Michael added. "If you hadn't assumed I killed him from the start, then you could have followed up on the investigation instead of gossip."

"I didn't…" she replied and sighed. "Taylor… the sheriff's deputy wouldn't fill me in. They all seem to think I did it."

Michael was quiet for a minute, and Lucy chided herself mentally. "I'm sorry," she apologized. "About breaking in... that was stupid, and..."

"Just stay out of my way henceforth," he said and walked out of the bakery. Alone, Lucy dropped into a chair and buried her face in her hands. The door opened again, and Michael walked in. Lucy raised her head when he said. "Sophie knew about Dennis' affair, but she did nothing about it. I was with her the night Dennis was killed, but that was only from ten pm. Before then I have no idea what she was up to, and I told the cops this."

"Why are you telling me this?"

Michael sighed and closed his eyes for a moment. Lucy watched as he sucked in a deep breath. "Because she's my friend, and..." his voice trailed off, and Lucy could tell it was difficult for him to get the words out. "Because she's my friend, and yet a part of me... A part of me doesn't know what she's capable of. When she found out about Dennis' affair, and that he had shipped her off to a nursing home out of town so he could have time to indulge in sleeping with his chef, she was enraged."

"Did you tell the cops this?" Lucy asked, her heart in her throat, and Michael nodded.

"It doesn't matter. Any woman who finds out her husband is cheating, has a right to be enraged. I just don't know how much she was willing to express her outrage."

Lucy spent the next day thinking about her conversation with Michael. His side of the story confused her, because she couldn't tell if he was saying the truth or trying to cover his tracks by throwing the blame and attention to Sophie.

———

LUCY CONVINCED Tricia to stay a week longer before she left town after she announced she had to get back to Stone Creek.

One evening, Lucy decided to check in on Sophie, so she drove to her house with Tricia. She had pondered on what Michael told her the last she saw him, and her curiosity made her make this trip to Sophie's house. Perhaps, if she struck up a conversation with Sophie, she might find out more.

Lucy knocked first and waited for a response. "Sophie?" she called and shifted her worried gaze to Tricia.

"I don't think anyone is home," Tricia whispered as Lucy touched the doorknob.

The door gave way and creaked as it opened, and Lucy jumped back. "Sophie?" she called again as she walked into the living room.

Inside the house was neatly arranged, the kitchen was spotless, and Lucy didn't think anyone made use of anything in there. "Sophie isn't here," she said as she swirled around the living room before her gaze landed on a door by the corner of the staircase leading upstairs. Lucy considered leaving the house with Tricia for a moment, but Michael's words suddenly flashed in her head.

I just don't know how far Sophie was willing to take hers.

What if Michael was telling the truth? She was in Sophie's house, and this was a chance to find anything that could help clear her name. She exhaled and shook her head, trying to dispel the idea, but when she opened her eyes again, her gaze landed on the door and she groaned.

"Tricia…" she started, but her aunt cut her words short.

"We should leave. Sophie isn't home," she said, and picked up a photo album on the center table. Tricia flipped the first page and an envelope fell out.

"What is it?" Lucy asked and rushed to her side.

"I think it's a letter," Tricia replied, and opened the envelope. She gasped after reading through it, and Lucy grabbed it from her and did the same.

"These are emails printed off from a computer... these seem to be from Diane," Lucy said. "She was blackmailing Dennis," she said as she read through the lines of texts and flipped over to the back page.

She read through the words quickly, then tossed them aside. "I think Sophie found out about his affair through these blackmails."

"Dennis was a jerk," Tricia commented and bent over to replace the envelope into the album on the table. They heard footsteps approach, and Lucy tensed.

"Not again," Tricia groaned.

"You think the cops caught us?" Lucy asked, and her questions were answered when the door swung open and Sophie stood in the doorway pointing a gun at them.

The smile on her face was cynical, and her eyes were bulging out of their sockets. It chilled Lucy to her bones.

"Surprised?" Sophie asked, and walked in.

Tricia backed away with Lucy, but Sophie stopped in front of them, then cocked and aimed the gun at Lucy. "I told you to stop digging."

It was Sophie all along? The break into her bakery, the car crash... she killed Dennis.

Lucy was standing face to face with a killer and she never expected that it would ever get to this. *Michael was right, she had taken it too far.*

"The cops have been following me for a while and I was expecting to leave town before anyone caught on to this mess," she continued.

"The mess you created when you killed your husband?"

She shook her head, and her eyes teared up. "I suffered and built everything we had with him, and he wanted to pay

me back by running off with some whore? He wasted everything we had on some stupid deal and when there was no
way out, he planned to shove some divorce papers down my
throat and hang me out to dry."

"So, you killed him, and left him in my backyard."

"He seemed to be obsessed with you the moment you
came to town. Forgive me if I thought he was repeating the
same cycle as he did with Diane. My husband never really
cared about anyone but himself, and you... you were just
collateral damage.

"I followed him the night he came to your place to speak
with you. But you had already locked up, so he went around
the property. That was my only chance, and I couldn't
waste it."

Lucy's heart was pounding so fast in her chest and when
she stole a glance at her aunt, she saw Tricia was sweating
with her arms raised above her head. Lucy turned back to
Sophie, who had taken off the bag hanging on her shoulder.

"I have to admit, you're brave, but not so smart. You
should have taken what Dennis offered and fled town, then
you wouldn't be in the center of all of this," she said and
laughed.

"You're a sick woman," Lucy retorted and her laughter
died.

"Really?" She asked, then fired the gun at Tricia. Lucy
screamed as the shot went off, and her aunt dropped to the
ground with a thud. Tears rushed out of her eyes as she
dropped beside her and screamed again.

"You killed her?" She yelled and reached for her aunt.
*What do I do? Please, don't die. This is all my fault? I shouldn't
have dragged you into this.*

"Aunt Tricia," she called, shaking her aunt as blood seeped
through her hands.

"She's probably not dead, but you will be in a few

minutes," Sophie boasted. "How sick is that?" she asked and cocked the gun again.

Lucy closed her eyes and waited to feel the pain as another shot went off again. *Was this the end?*

13

*L*ucy was still alive. She could feel her heart beating. Was it a dream? Had Sophie actually shot her aunt? She couldn't tell because it was like she was floating.

It felt like she was in a trance, but the screaming ambulance, the faint voices of the cops talking to each other, proved it wasn't.

"Miss Hale?" a voice called, dragging her from her thoughts, and she rubbed her eyes. "Are you alright?" the cop asked, and she nodded, her throat too dry to speak.

Two cops wheeled her aunt on a gurney out of the house, and Tricia winked at her. For a moment, she thought she lost the only family member she had left. But Tricia was alive, and the ambulance rushed her to the hospital while Taylor drove Lucy to the station in his car.

As she sat in front of him after giving her statement, she waited for his usual scolding, but none came. His lips pressed into a tight line. He handed over a bottle of water, which Lucy accepted..

"We were handling it," he said to her. "I placed cops to watch Sophie's every move, and I was carrying out a full investigation. What you did was reckless and stupid, and you could have gotten yourself killed."

She blinked and said nothing. Her mind was still reeling from everything that had happened.

Taylor sighed and ordered a cop to take her to the hospital. When Lucy walked into the room where her aunt was, she broke down crying when she saw her lying on the hospital bed, awake.

"I thought you were dead," she shrieked out and Tricia forced a smile.

"She got my shoulder, but I recorded her on my phone. There's no way she's escaping her crimes."

Lucy exhaled and sat beside her on the bed, then took her hands. "Thank you so much," she sobbed. She couldn't have gotten through this without her aunt's support, and she couldn't be more grateful than she already was.

"I love you, Lucy, and you're my little girl," Tricia said as they hugged. "You will always be my little girl."

Tricia got discharged four days later, and Lucy prepared a celebratory dinner. Hannah made the meal; chicken soup and pasta, and they dined in the bakery that evening together. It felt like a huge weight had been lifted off her shoulder, and with Sophie in police custody, Lucy felt safe in Ivy Creek for the first time since she returned.

"I think I'm out of my depth here," she said to Tricia later that evening as they cleaned up the dishes. "Running the bakery, trying to expand. Maybe it was too much to handle too soon."

"You're quitting?" Tricia asked, and she shrugged.

"I had a job in Denver, a life I left to be here. Maybe I need to get back to that instead of trying so hard to start something here."

"That's sad," Tricia replied. "You make such a delicious double crust fruit pie, and if I think that, then I'm sure others do as well. Give it time, now that the killer has been found, they'll come around," she advised, and her words gave Lucy a fresh jolt of hope. "You could start something new here, and make it something solid, something to hold onto. Besides… I can always eat all the pie you bake," she joked, and they both laughed as Lucy locked the doors and they headed up to the apartment above the bakery.

Tricia had a point. She could start a new life here in Ivy Creek. She had found a way to stand on her feet and persist against the odds, and Lucy had never been as optimistic about anything as she was about the bakery.

She wanted this. It was why she opted to stay back at first, and life in the city might never be enough for her again. Not when she knew she could start something new here.

14

hree weeks later, it was as if Lucy had never been at the center of a murder investigation. There was a long line in front of the Sweet Delights' concession store, and Lucy had to trade places with her newly hired chef, Diane Keen. Lucy had hired Diane because she had skills best suited for a bakery and not an art store. She had a full schedule today at the bakery with Hannah as they prepared to deliver a wedding cake contract.

When she arrived at the bakery, the lemon summer berry cake they baked together stood tall on the counter. It was ready to be delivered, and Lucy smiled as she took out her phone and took shots of it for her blog. She still uploaded posts every week, and she had started a new trend that involved different recipes for every Tuesday. She called it *The Tues-delight.*

"It's amazing, right?" Hannah asked, and she nodded. "I've asked the delivery van to be here, so we can both take this to the venue."

"I think I'll add this lemon berry cake to the new menu.

It's really nice, and would gain a lot of attention," Lucy suggested and Hannah agreed with her.

"Personally, I think I might come to prefer it over the regular cakes we sell."

"What time is the wedding?" Lucy asked, and Hannah glanced at her watch.

"Ten am, that's exactly one hour from now," she replied with a sigh. "I better get changed," she added, then turned around and dashed up the stairs leading to Lucy's apartment.

Whistling to herself, Lucy grabbed a napkin from the stand and wiped out the counter, then went into the kitchen. She heard the front door open, so she walked back out to greet the customer with a happy smile.

Taylor stood on the other end of her counter, and beside him was a face she hadn't seen in a long time. "Dylan?" she called, and Taylor's younger brother laughed. "Oh, my God," she exclaimed, then walked around the table to wrap her arms around his neck. "When did you get back?"

"Few days ago, and I've already heard the gossip about this place," he commented and looked around. "Had to come see for myself."

"I'm glad you came," she said and her gaze moved to Taylor, who stood quietly and watched the happy reunion. After Dennis' case was resolved, and Sophie was found out to be his killer, Lucy had left town for a few days to wrap up her life in the city and tender her resignation to the publishing house officially. When she returned, she had rushed back into business.

She now ran the only bakery in town as Sophie had sold out Spring's bakery before she was arrested, and Diane Keen had decided to stay in town and keep her pregnancy after Sophie was caught.

"Hey," she said to Taylor when his brother wandered away to look around the bakery. Lucy had added more artwork to the walls and changed the wallpaper to give the place a fresh look. And so far, everything seemed perfect.

"Hi," Taylor replied, his gaze fixed on hers.

For a moment, Lucy forgot all about their feud and was about to thank him for helping her out with the case.

"I see you stuck around," he said and looked around the bakery.

She shrugged. "I did. Turns out running a bakery is fun and I don't get to do that in the big city," she replied with a smile, and their gaze met for a moment. She looked away first, and when he said nothing else, she added. "Thank you, for helping with Dennis' case."

Lucy turned towards Dylan. "Now that you're back, we're going to have so much fun," she said and wrapped her arm around his shoulder, grateful she had an old friend around again.

"Just like old times," Dylan added, and the duo laughed.

Hannah came down a few minutes later, fully dressed for the wedding, and it was Lucy's turn to dash up the stairs and get ready for the long day ahead.

When she got back down, Dylan and Taylor had left, and Lucy joined Hannah in attending to the fresh stream of customers in the bakery.

"I would like a tart, please," a lady said when she walked over to the counter, and Lucy gave her brightest smile as she reached into the display glass for a lemon tart. Sales had improved drastically in the last three weeks and Lucy hoped it was the beginning of better days.

The End

AFTERWORD

Thank you for reading Which Pie Goes with Murder? I really hope you enjoyed reading it as much as I had writing it!

If you have a minute, please consider leaving a review on Amazon or the retailer where you got it.

Many thanks in advance for your support!

TWINKLE, TWINKLE, DEADLY SPRINKLES

CHAPTER 1 SNEAK PEEK

CHAPTER 1 SNEAK PEEK

*I*t was a sunny afternoon, and the birds chirping in the sky above reminded Lucy of a time when she played on the patio while her parents worked in the bakery. She had grown up happy, her hours spent learning recipes from her mother's cookbook, and holidays full of entertaining events like the summer kid's camp and marathon races. Those fond memories she held unto filled her leisure time.

She sighed when the door behind her opened, and Hannah, her employee, and friend walked out, holding two glasses. "Freshly made orange juice," Hannah said, smiling as Lucy took the glass.

"Thanks," Lucy replied, and took a sip. Hannah settled into a chair close to Lucy's and took out a notepad from her apron's pocket. "Have you made a list of the needed items?"

Hannah pushed the notepad to Lucy. "We have a week to the delivery date, so we should get them tomorrow, then we begin preparations."

This spring, she had registered more deals than she had since the bakery re-opened, and there was more to come. She was certain of it. Lucy took out a pen from her shirt's pocket and scribbled down additional flavors used for daily baking sales and fruit additives.

She was trying out a new recipe by the end of spring, and if she perfected it in time, it would be a summer addition for their menu. "Thank you, Hannah," she said after making the notes. "I should get them by tomorrow."

Hannah placed both her hands on the table, and Lucy sipped her juice again as her friend's gaze landed on hers.

"Have you heard?" she asked, clearing her throat.

Hannah was Lucy's source for town gossip. She lived downtown, and since Lucy remained in the apartment upstairs, she barely had contact with the citizens of Ivy Creek unless they came to Sweet Delights.

"Heard?"

"About the merger." Hannah's eyes widened as she continued. "It's the talk of the town. Philip Anderson Accountants bought a subsidiary accounting firm, and merged them into one, and this is the third time in two years he's poached some small firm."

Lucy was aware of Philip Anderson, the town's biggest accounting firm owned by Roland Anderson, one of the town's founding members. She had never done business with him, but he had a lot of clout in town.

"Some say his wife got him the deal," Hannah continued. "I think they worked hand in hand on every acquisition, but the glory goes to the husband every time."

As Hannah talked, Lucy spotted a red mustang approaching. The driver stopped and parked by the corner of the street, and when the door opened, a lady stepped out.

"That's Mrs. Anderson," Hannah announced in a shaky voice, and Lucy saw her cheeks turn red.

Blushing, Hannah excused herself and scurried into the

bakery. Lucy watched as Mrs. Anderson walked towards the patio with short, calculated steps.

What were the odds that they were just talking about her and she came here? Or what did she want?

Lucy shook the thoughts away and rose to her feet when Mrs. Anderson got to the patio.

Slowly, she took off the shades she wore. "Hi," she greeted in a silky tone, and extended a hand. "Becky Anderson."

Lucy accepted the extended hand and smiled.

"Lucy, right?" Becky asked, skipping formalities, and Lucy nodded.

"Yes," she replied, and her gaze traveled over Becky. She noticed her well-manicured red painted nails, and the neat crimson colored suit she wore. "Please, seat," she offered, and Becky sat. "Is there something you need?"

Becky smiled. The corners of her lips curved, and the sides of her eyes wrinkled. "Of course, dear," she replied. "I wouldn't drive all the way out here if I didn't." Her gaze dropped to the gold watch on her slender wrists for a second and when she raised it again, Lucy met her deep velvety brown eyes.

"My husband, and I are hosting a charity event next weekend, and I need services for baked treats," she continued. "I always hire the very best, and I've…" She took a slight pause, and her gaze traveled around the patio. "I've heard you're good at what you do," she added when her gaze landed on Lucy. Becky smiled again. "Are you?"

Lucy chose not to answer the last question. With a deep sigh, she linked her fingers on her lap and replied. "I would like to know what you have in mind for the treats, your budget, and of course, guest list."

Becky reached into her designer purse, took out a piece of paper, and handed it over to Lucy. "I've made a list of all that to make our alliance easy. Everything you'll need is written here."

Lucy scanned the notes on the paper and frowned. "There's no budget. A budget plays a role, as it helps us work smoothly," she explained, and dropped the paper. "You should state a budget which, of course, includes my pay for the event."

Lucy raised her chin, determined not to let Becky's intimidating presence bait her. She could handle business deals and she was every bit as professional as Becky Anderson.

Becky chuckled softly. "Like I mentioned earlier, it's a charity event. Surely you know what charity events are?"

"I do…"

"That's great," Becky interrupted. "You offer your services for free, just as I am hosting the event to gather proceedings for charity. My husband and I do this every year, and this year we're trying to raise more… for a good cause."

Lucy pressed her lips together, but Becky's gaze remained persistent as she continued. "If you agree to do this, of course you will gain the right amount of publicity for your bakery. As director of the local chamber of commerce, I will have many guests in attendance who are all potential clients of yours with the right recommendation."

Lucy analyzed her offer quietly as she stared at the list of treats needed and the number of guests. *Over two hundred guests meant some were non-locals. It was definitely going to be a major event.*

"I take it you're thinking about my offer," Becky said after a minute of silence. She waved her hand as she continued. "There are a few potential clients on my list I can hand over to you right now once you agree to this deal."

"What's in it for you?" Lucy asked. "Seems like you're offering more than you'll be receiving."

Becky shrugged. "Let's just say I have a knack for helping people," she replied.

Lucy sighed, and the smug grin on Becky's face widened when she said. "Fine, I'll do it."

Becky clapped her hands together. "This will be fun," she murmured, took out a pen and scribbled her contact details on the paper. "I will expect a call from you."

Lucy watched her walk away after that and rubbed her forehead. "Did you just agree to work an event for free?" Hannah asked, stepping out of the bakery. "I heard the entire conversation," she added when Lucy raised her brows. Hannah pulled out a chair and sat. "You let her bait you."

"She offered excellent prospects," Lucy replied. "More clients… cooperate and wealthy clients if I work on this, and what's best part is I get to meet them in person. Isn't that great?" she asked, as if in doubt of her decision. She had heard rumors about the Andersons' and their need for perfection. There was constant gossip surrounding them, revolving around Becky Anderson's short temper, and the need to stay in control. She wondered if working for the woman was a right choice.

If their alliance didn't turn out as planned, she would offer compensation, right? She rubbed her jaw again and looked at Hannah. "You think it's a good deal? Considering you know all about Becky Anderson through the gossips."

"It's a great deal. Working for Mrs. Anderson shouldn't be that hard," Hannah replied. "But you don't sound so sure… do you think you made a wrong decision?"

"I don't know." They both fell silent, and Lucy added. "I have a weird gut feeling about it though, and I have to admit, she's quite intimidating," she said as an image of Becky's cool smile flashed in her head.

"I think it will be huge," Hannah exclaimed, and the excitement in her eyes brought a smile to Lucy's face. She pushed down the tingle that had formed in the pit of her stomach and blamed it on over-analysis.

Lucy grinned and handed over the paper she held to Hannah. "Here's a list of the treats needed," she said. "We will start work immediately."

Hannah walked back into the bakery after their brief conversation, and Lucy relaxed in her chair and sighed. This was a new prospect for her, and it could lead to another expansion in her business. "You've come a long way, Lucy," she murmured, and exhaled again as she raised her head and shut her eyes, mentally congratulating herself on her accomplishments.

But why did it feel like there was another wave of trouble coming and something was about to go wrong?

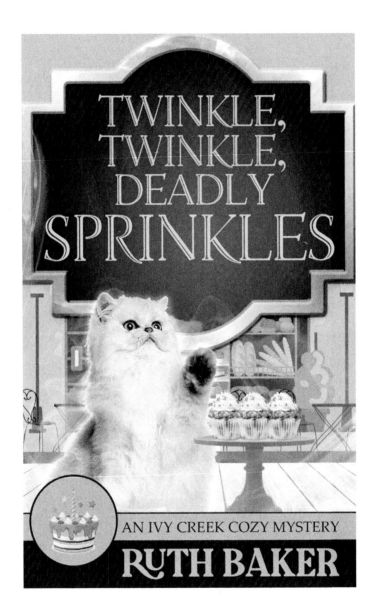

TWINKLE, TWINKLE, DEADLY SPRINKLES

AN IVY CREEK COZY MYSTERY

RUTH BAKER

ALSO BY RUTH BAKER

The Ivy Creek Cozy Mystery Series

Which Pie Goes with Murder? (Book 1)

Twinkle, Twinkle, Deadly Sprinkles (Book 2)

Waffles and Scuffles (Book 3)

Silent Night, Unholy Bites (Book 4)

NEWSLETTER SIGNUP

Want **FREE** COPIES OF FUTURE **CLEANTALES** BOOKS, FIRST NOTIFICATION OF NEW RELEASES, CONTESTS AND GIVEAWAYS?

GO TO THE LINK BELOW TO SIGN UP TO THE NEWSLETTER!

https://cleantales.com/newsletter/